# Overheard In A Graveyard

# Overheard In A Graveyard

## Susan Price

*Cover Art: Andrew Price*

*Other Ghost Story Collections*

*by Susan Price*

Hauntings

Nightcomers

# CONTENTS

## Overheard In A Graveyard

What is longing made of, that it never wears out?

Bone breaks. Rock wears away to sand. In this dark rain, hard iron falls to rust.

Razors blunt, but longing's edge still cuts deep.

If you'd gone to another land, I could have followed, by road, by ship.

But no path will lead me to you, no door will let me through to you. There's no wall I can climb, no thorns I can fight through—

How can you be so far from me?

What is longing made of, that there's more comfort in a bed of stone, a thorn-pillow, sheets of ice?

*Who weeps on my grave, who keeps me from sleep?*

*Is it you who unearths me to this cold rain, this dark, this wind and all this grief?*

*My bed was made; I lie in it. Hard frosts have cracked my bones. Down the rain has come and seeped me through. Twelve long months have past and gone since I was warm and quick.*

*Go away love.*

*Leave me to the grave.*

I can see you!

I can see you.

Can I touch you?

Let me hold you again. I Never held any like I held you. There was never any touched me like you. Never since.

Can I rest my head on yours? Will you lay your head on my shoulder?

I want to hold you, warm—

*I'm warm no more.*

I'll warm you.

*Ah, love. If I put my arms around you now, if I pressed me close to you now…*

*Ah, love, your heart would catch and stop cold.*

*Go in from the rain now, and warm yourself.*

*In twelve months more you'll love some other— and love the more for losing me.*

*You store up grief, love - but never fear you'll miss your share of grief.*

*Get in from the wind, love.*

*Leave me to the grave.*

Kiss me goodbye, then. One kiss.

*My mouth is cold as the wet clay. My breath earthy strong.*

*Go ask a kiss from a warmer mouth with sweeter breath than mine.*

*Go in from the cold, love.*

*Leave me to the grave.*

I want to be with you.

Let me stay.

Is there room in that little house for me? Take me in out of the rain. Let me hug you close— then there'll be room.

Let me in, please let me in. I'd sooner lie with you in that deep bed than stand under the sun and long for you.

*There is no room.*
   *Go from here now— you keep me from sleep!*
   *Your every tear's a chain that holds me here; ever sob a stone that weighs me down.*
   *Have some thought of me!— and turn your back and go, and leave me to the grave.*

I think of you, I always think of you!
   Forget, forget! Don't I try? I am hugging burning ice— wouldn't I lose it if I could?
   What is grief made of, that it never blunts? A steel trap loses its jaws, but grief's a trap that won't lose me. If gnawing through my own wrist would set me free, I'd gnaw my hand off!
   Let me in to you, let me in out of the rain.

*Is this love, to unearth me to this pain? Go from me, leave me, let me sleep.*

I shall lie on your grave and howl your name. I shall weep dry earth to mud. I'll call and call your name until you come. Every night I'll howl you to me, every night, every night and all.
   I never owned a thing but I shared it with you, never a thought, never a coin I had but I shared it with you - and now we'll share this grief, I swear, while the trap bites on me it shall bite on you.
   Let me hold you. I was never held by any like you held me. I never held any since like I held you. Let me warm you, love.

*Come to me, then, come here to me, love.*
   *What? now you draw back?*
   *Don't you love me any more?*

Cold— !

*Hush now, hush, don't fear. Our bed's unaired, it's chill and damp- but it'll warm, it'll warm as I draw you in.*

But so cold—

# AUTHOR'S NOTE TO 'OVERHEARD IN A GRAVEYARD.'

I know almost the exact moment this story leaped into my head.

I've always been fascinated by folklore, and I knew there were many ballads and legends about ghosts returning to beg mourners to stop grieving and let them rest in peace.

I had been turning over in my head the idea of writing my own version of this story, but couldn't find a way to do it.

I was watching the film *'Silent Tongue'* and was surprised to find that it told a version of this story too. In the film a simple boy has been married, by his father, to a Native American woman. When she dies, he is distraught.

According to her customs, her body has been given a 'sky-burial' — wrapped in a blanket and lodged in the branches of a tree, to be eaten by birds. Unable to bear this, the boy sits beneath the tree with a shotgun, driving away everything that approaches.

Eventually his wife's ghost appears and berates him for hindering her passage to the next world. (It's a great scene in a great film.)

Perhaps it was the influence of the film with its pared down dialogue, but I suddenly saw how to write my version— pare it down to nothing but the words of the ghost and mourner.

Cut all description of surroundings— let the title alone tell the reader what kind of scene they were to imagine.

Cut out all pronouns, and then the ghost could be male or female— or the same sex as the mourner. It's for the reader to decide.

# CRUEL MOTHER

*She leaned her back against a thorn*
*All alone and so lonely...*

She leaned her back against a cheap chest of drawers, and she sweated, her body heaved, she grunted, begged aloud for it to be over, sobbed...

*There her baby she has borne*
*For ever and ever lonely.*

The thing that had forced its way out of her lay on the grubby carpet, covered in blood and yuck, like an alien. It scared her. She hated it.

Before she'd had time to rest, or think, or do anything, it started again, and she thought she was having another one— but it was just another load of yuck. Horrible. A real mess. She'd have to wash her clothes— clean the carpet— and it'd never come out. How to explain it? It was all that thing's fault.

No one knew she was up the duff. She hadn't known herself until— she didn't know how long ago. She didn't keep track of time much, except for pay-day. Time passed, whether you bothered about it or not.

The women at work had been talking, and she'd remembered things she'd heard said in the past, and it had all come together so she'd woken up one night, thinking: *Fuck! I'm lumbered!* It wasn't just that she'd missed a couple of months.

Nobody else knew. Nobody had said anything— and they would, if they'd noticed, you could be sure of that. They'd love the chance. No— she was fat, and her work overall was shapeless. They couldn't tell.

"Yo'm porking it on," Marianne said to her one day. "Who et all the pies, eh?" No one else said anything.

She hadn't gone to the doctor or anything. A lot of the time she just forgot about it— she was good at forgetting. She'd remember it, sweating, in the night. Her hope was that it would go away. It happened sometimes. She might be lucky.

Please— let it just go away.

She'd pinned all her hopes on it just going away.

Babbies... Didn't they have to be reported? You had to tell the Government about them. She didn't know how you did that, didn't know where you had to go, which buses to catch, what the opening times were— didn't know anything and panicked at the thought of having to find out. She didn't know what questions they'd ask her. She wouldn't know the right answer, she was sure of that. Never did, never had.

Nurses came poking around when you had a babby, reporting on you. Telling you what to do. Giving you grief. And you had to keep buying things, and she never had enough money to get through the week. You had to look after babbies, and she didn't know how to do that, didn't want to do that, day after day, every day. Trouble. Lumber. Grief.

It was making a noise, the thing, the babby. It'd get her thrown out.

How was she supposed to work, if she had to look after that? She wouldn't have money for her stuff.

*She took a knife so keen and sharp*
*All alone and so lonely*
*She pierced it through its tender heart*
*For ever and ever so lonely.*

The packing-knife from work was in the pocket of her overalls. She was always forgetting it and bringing it home with her. It was really sharp, and you could pull the blade out, make it longer. It was only like sticking a knife in a piece of chicken, and a bit more blood didn't make any difference. She wrapped the thing and the other yuck in her towel, so she didn't have to see it. Then she crawled onto the bed and went to sleep.

It was still there when she woke. The towel it was wrapped it was soaked, and there was a big stain on the carpet too. She felt lousy—and she'd missed a shift at work. Lost a night's wages.

She put on her coat, and nipped down the hall to the bathroom. It was empty, and nobody knocked on the door while she was bathing. Afterwards, she put her coat back on over her wet body, hurried back to her room, and dried herself on her bed-sheet, because she only had the one towel.

She stood looking at the mess, and the thing wrapped in the towel. If she could get rid of it, she could have her towel back, though she'd have to wash it. Again. Another load of washing when she'd already paid for one that week.

The thing had to be got rid of. Couldn't leave it there.

She found a plastic bag to put it in, from a bundle she had in the corner of the kitchenette, but then couldn't bear to unwrap the towel. The idea was to get rid of it, not look at it.

In the end, she stuffed the whole squashy, smelly bundle, towel and all, into the bag. She dressed, put on her damp coat, picked up the bag, and went out. It wasn't pleasant, walking. She was sore.

*She buried it under the marble stone*
*All alone and so lonely.*

Her room was one of three above a takeaway. It was evening as she went down the steps into the street. Lights glared from shops and restaurants. Cars hissed through the puddles.

She didn't go as far as she'd intended to go. Too sore. She turned down the side of the Kashmir, went into the yard where the big bins were. Lifting the lid of one, she tossed the bag inside. She could tell from the noise it made that the bin was half-empty, and that the bag had fallen deep inside. It would never be noticed or found.

*Then she turned and went on home*
*For ever and ever lonely*

Then she turned and went to work. Couldn't afford any more time off: rent to pay and ciggies to buy. She went into the store by the back way, punching in the code, and took the goods-lift upstairs, leaving her coat in the ladies. A couple of people said hello to her, but she only nodded. She still felt weak, and shivery, and sore down there.

"Nice of you to let us know you weren't coming in," the manager said.

"Sorry. Had a bit of a bug."

"Yeah," he said. "The kind that comes in a bottle, I bet."

She trudged off to her work without answering.

The lighting was dim, especially in the aisles at the edges of the supermarket, where the the shelves held what the manager called the 'less value-added stock.' Not many people wandered in during the night, and they got in the way of the shelf-stocking and never bought much, so why encourage them by having the lights at full strength?

Sounds drifted over from other aisles: the squeak of a skip's wheel, the thump of a cardboard box, the sharp din of a can dropped on tiles. Occasionally someone spoke, or called out, or laughed, but the words were indistinct. No music played. She worked the aisle of cleaning materials, and thought glumly that, earlier, she could have done with some big rubbish bags and strong cleaners. The carpet in her flat was starting to stink.

She'd take the packing-knife home again, and use it to cut the stained section of the carpet out, and throw it away. The landlord would create hell if he found out, but she wouldn't be telling him.

At the far end of the aisle something low down, near the floor, peeped round the edge of a loaded skip.

*As she walked out one moonlit night*
*All alone and so lonely*
*She saw a babe all dressed in white*
*For ever and ever lonely.*

Peeped, then ducked away.

Her heart clenched tight, stopped, tipped over into its next thump. She brushed her hand over her eyes. The light was dim, yellowish... She hadn't seen—

Forget it.

She opened boxes with the packing knife, the cardboard crunching. Pierced through that tender heart... Stooping and heaving, her body aching, she shifted the packs of bottles and cans to the floor, before stacking the individual cartons on the shelves. She worked for an age, and ten minutes passed.

Turning back to the skip, she flinched from the baby sitting on the drab boxes, and saw it melt into shadows of torn polythene, lettering and logos.

*Oh babe, oh babe, if you were mine,*
*All alone and so lonely*
*I'd dress you up in silk so fine*
*For ever and ever so lonely*

She heaved down the box of washing-up liquids, and slit the polythene with her knife. Her heart pounded, she sweated, as she stacked them in the shelf. *Fuck off,* she told the baby. *You're in the skip, and you're staying there. I'm saying nothing.*

Had somebody found it, though? Had somebody gone into the skip, had her landlord gone into her room and found the mess?

She calmed her heart, knowing they hadn't. Nobody would root through a skip of stinking rubbish, and the landlord had never gone into her room before. He only wanted the rent. If he went into the room, he might have to admit that the oven didn't work, and the roof leaked.

Nobody knew. Keep quiet, forget it, and nobody would find out.

Forget. Nothing to gain by remembering.

At break she went out the back, into the delivery bay, stood in the damp chill, in the dark, and smoked a couple of ciggies. She needed them. The baby sat on the wall at the back of the bay, and waved its hands at her.

*Oh mother oh mother when I was yours*
*All alone and so lonely*
*You dressed me in my own heart's blood*
*For ever and ever so lonely*

She stared it down. *Think yourself lucky, you little bugger. You're better off where you are. Never gave you away to strangers, did I? Never pushed off and left you to whoever. You'll never have to go through that. And what's there to look forward to? More of the same. Believe me, Bab, being alive aint what it's cracked up to be. You're lucky. Be grateful.*

When her shift ended, in the dark of early morning, she went home with a half-bottle of the cheapest vodka, staff discount. There was no way the little bugger was keeping her awake.

Lying on her back, painkillers taken, her breaths rattled her throat, pausing, choking, reverberating at the back of her nose... In sleep, in blurry, drunken, unresting sleep, she wandered dark streets and hillsides...

*Babe oh babe come tell me true*
*All alone and so lonely*
*What penance must I serve for you?*
*For ever and ever so lonely*

11

*For seven years you shall ring the bell*
*All alone and so lonely*
*For seven years you will wait in Hell*
*For ever and ever so lonely*

When she woke the next afternoon, she was ill. A dully pounding, throbbing head, a sick stomach, joints aching like an old woman's. She drank tea, and watched television, and thought about how bad she felt. In the evening, she dragged herself out to work, and then she had work to think about.

There was something— something big, something bad— something that had happened, or that she'd done, or that had been done to her... It lowered at the edges of memory, but she wouldn't look at it, wouldn't concentrate... Plenty of bad and hurtful things had happened. She'd become good at not remembering.

Cider was cheaper than vodka. It made sure she slept, even when she had to keep waking to stumble out to the bathroom. Coming back, she keeled onto the bed and was asleep again, grunting, snoring...

*Oh mother, mother, come hark to me,*
*All alone and so lonely...*

*Author's Note on 'The Cruel Mother.'*

This is another story based on a folk-ballad.

I was in the gym, on the treadmill, listening to June Tabor's recording of *The Cruel Mother.'*

It came to me in an instant that I should write the story in a modern setting, with the haunting refrains of the old ballad threading through it.

# THE FOOTSTEPS ON THE STAIRS

The truth of it is, my mother and father should never have married.

I think my father would have managed to be miserable, no matter what; and would have made whoever was around him miserable; but my mother could have made a perfectly ordinary, dull, happy marriage. And her children would have been happy too. Though, of course, if she'd married someone else, I suppose her children wouldn't have been my brothers and me.

One of my parents' problems was money. My mother was rather well off. Both sides of her family were in business— her father's side made all sorts of boiled sugar sweets, which were sold in big jars in little shops all over the country— cough-sweets and humbugs and lemon-drops and all that. Her mother's side rewound electrical motors, the kind that drove factory machinery and generators. So my mother had trust-funds and income from capital and shares and bonds and what not.

My father's family were a rackety lot who never seemed to have a penny between them. They were always in debt, and borrowing from people, and then forgetting that they'd borrowed. Or not bothering to remember, depending on how you looked at it. Father had been an actor before the war— the Second World War, that is, darling. I think they married because of the war. A lot of people did. If it hadn't been for the war, my father would probably just have been a fling for my mother. She would have been mad about him for a while, then tired of his unreliability, and married someone respectable.

But instead the war came along while she was still at the 'mad about him' stage. And, oh, my dear! We might all be killed tomorrow! Let's get married! So they did.

My father had a mixed war. He joined the army, and was bored to death by drill and barracks, but I don't think he ever saw action except on film-sets. Because, of course, he was an actor; and someone or other decided that he could serve the war effort best by making films to keep Britain's collective pecker up. So you can still see my father, even now, on morning and afternoon television, being awfully brave and stiff-upper-lipped as a fireman, or a sailor adrift in an open boat, or a chirpy young soldier on leave on an underground station platform. 'Do your worst, old Hitler!' All that sort of stuff. I don't think he ever starred in anything.

Meanwhile, my mother was mostly with her family, somewhere in Northamptonshire, being told she was a silly girl who'd made a big mistake, that she'd regret. Well, you can imagine the effect of that.

After the war, they had a honeymoon— both a real honeymoon, a fortnight in Scotland, and a time when they were wrapped up in each other, and doted on each other.

From what I've been told by aunts and uncles and people, I think it lasted about two years. I was born about half way through it.

After that— I don't know if it's true to say my father was bored. You could say he was restless, I suppose, and it would amount to the same thing. Or resentful, perhaps. Or all of these things. Anyway, he started taking off. He'd go out in the morning to buy a newspaper and not come back for three days. At first, of course, my mother was frantic. Had he had an accident? Was he dead, in hospital, lying hurt somewhere? She'd try to find him, phoning hospitals and friends and the police. She'd put me in my pram and search the district on foot.

My father, of course, was perfectly well, and enjoying himself in a pub somewhere; or he'd gone to see a friend in another city and was dossing on their floor; or he'd 'suddenly fancied a day at the seaside.'

He'd come strolling back in after however many days it was, apparently expecting a welcome, or pretending that he did, and, of course, there'd be a screaming row. Where had he been?— He didn't have to explain himself to her, her family or their money.— Didn't he know how he'd worried her?— Only a stupid neurotic cow like her would worry about a grown man taking a few days for himself. And so on.

My father was still following his 'acting career'. He'd get a theatre job, or a part in a radio play, a bit part in a film— and we were all supposed to be joyful and celebrate. And then he'd be resting for months. His disappearances often coincided with his losing a job. "I didn't want to come home to a lot of long faces, so I went to the races." For a week.

"You lost your job again, so you threw money away on horses?" That would be my mother.

"Never mind the money. You've got plenty." But don't think my father was made to feel inadequate by all my mother's money, and feel sorry for him. Later, when he was with another woman who didn't have a penny to bless herself with, he behaved in just the same way, but he had another excuse.

Every now and again my parents would come together again, and we'd all be very happy for a while. As a child, I had no idea why these comings-togethers and fallings-apart happened. They just did. My brothers were conceived during these periods of 'new beginnings' and 'sorting out our problems'— but born during times of screaming rows and crying jags.

My mother started relying on herself more and more. She paid the bills, and managed our household solely on her own money with, I think, some help from her father. Our family began to be my mother and her children— and occasionally there was this male visitor who crashed in for a few days, and was sometimes fun, and sometimes a pain.

I don't really know when I became aware of all this, but I was about eleven, I think, when I started picking up talk of a divorce. My mother had had enough. "My parents were right," she said. "I admit it. Too bloody late, but I admit it."

At about the same time she inherited, from her grandmother, a cottage near the sea, in Dorset. We'd go and live there, my mother decided, us boys and her. It would be a better life for all of us. I started day-dreaming about days on the beach, and swimming in the sea, and perhaps there'd be enough money for a pony? I looked forward to it.

I wasn't at all happy when I heard my father being included in the plans. I remember saying to my brothers that he'd just let us down again. We'd got used to him promising to take us to the cinema, or be at our birthday parties, and then not turning up. "I forgot all about it!" he would say, and would slap his own head, expecting us to laugh, but we stopped laughing after a few years. He never forgot what he wanted to remember.

He made a huge fuss once because he turned up to take us to a pantomime, and I wasn't ready. I was lying on my bed in my old clothes, reading a book. When it was demanded of me why I hadn't changed, I said, "I didn't think you'd turn up." I genuinely didn't think he would. I'd considered changing, but was bored at the thought of going to all that trouble for nothing, so I hadn't bothered.

Father gave a better performance than anything in the pantomime, stamping around our house, declaring how unappreciative and selfish we were, not caring how we wasted his time. He had a very cold audience. By that time, even my younger brothers weren't impressed.

So a new life by the sea with Father? We knew it would never happen.

But Father convinced mother somehow. I think she saw it as yet another new way of fixing him, of making him what she wanted. The cottage she'd inherited needed a lot of work, and her idea was that we'd all move there, as a family, for the summer holidays, and live there while the place was done up. She and Father would both muck in with the work they could do, and in working together they'd get to know each other all over again; and my father would oversee the work that had to be done by tradesmen. It would give him a sense of responsibility and achievement that would be good for him; and he would be with his family. I don't know if she said this to my father. She certainly said it to me and my grandmother.

Perhaps Father was sincere, and really did want to start over with us again. Maybe he was aghast at the idea of not having a place to bring his laundry, or someone who'd feed him and give him a bed when nobody else would. Perhaps he wanted a foot in the door of this holiday cottage by the sea.

Or am I being too cynical? Possibly.

He certainly stayed with us for longer than usual without suddenly taking off, and he worked steadily on the cottage... I think he enjoyed the work, found it a novelty. Knocking down walls, digging earth away from brickwork, planing down doors. I even began to like him, rather. He was good company. I often think that if I'd known him as a friend, and not as a father, I would have wholeheartedly liked him. If all you ask of a friend is that they be good company while you're with them, you can easily overlook the way they treat other people, even if you disapprove of it. It's harder to forgive a father.

Mother had the whole kitchen ripped out, and one of the bedrooms upstairs turned into a bathroom, and living in the place soon became impossible. There was nowhere to cook, and thick brick and plaster dust was everywhere and got into everything. So she asked about the village, and found a small place to rent— a tiny house, not very comfortable, but it had a kitchen and bedrooms, which were our main requirement. So we breakfasted at the house, walked into the village and spent all day at the cottage. We children either did what we could to help, or ran errands, or played on the beach and generally roamed around, much as we would have done on any holiday. At intervals we showed up at the cottage to see what was going on, or to complain that we were hungry. It was all working very well, when my mother had a telegram telling her that her older sister was seriously ill.

More telegrams and phone calls followed— mobile phones didn't exist in those days. It was quite difficult to telephone Yorkshire from a tiny Dorset village, believe me. First you had to find a phone you could use, then calls had to be relayed, from operator to operator. Luckily, the larger of the village pubs had a phone. The outcome of all the fuss was that my mother packed her bags and vamoosed for Yorkshire, for an indeterminate time.

The cottage and our welfare was left entirely in my father's hands. Was this another stage in my father's re-habilitation? 'Let's see if he can rise to the occasion and take responsibility.' Perhaps. But Aunt Marjorie *was* very ill— she'd had a stroke— so it may have been simple desperation.

Mother did say to me, "You're old enough now. If you need me, you can telephone from the pub or the post office. And you know you can ask anyone for help." Which was true. Mother had made a lot of friends in the village. So, she wasn't relying entirely on Father.

During Mother's absence, our days went on much as before. I returned more often to the cottage at first, because I fully expected to find that Father had up and left us, and that I had to go through the dreaded business of asking for help and telephoning Mother. But to my surprise, Father not only stayed around, he worked on the cottage with greater energy than before. If he did leave, it was to visit suppliers or hunt up tradesmen, and he returned with tales of what he'd achieved. "It's nice to not have your mother breathing down our necks, isn't it?" he said to me once. I remember, because it made me feel so angry on mother's behalf and, at the same time, so much his pal.

It was the nights that changed. When Mother had been there, we'd gone back to the house she'd rented, and eaten, and then she'd stayed with us through the evening, while we played board games or read, or quarrelled. She saw us to bed and, we knew she was downstairs, writing letters, doing accounts, or reading, until she came up to bed herself.

Father, meanwhile, was in the village pub. He'd worked all day, to his way of thinking, he'd earned a night in the pub. He might come home at any hour.

But while Mother was away, was Father still going to spend every evening in the pub? I knew that my younger brothers were worried about being left alone at night in this little house on the edge of the village.

"What if Murderers come?" my youngest brother asked once. He seemed to have some idea that murdering was a profession, and that bands of murderers roamed about the country, ever on the look-out for a chance to practice their craft. When I read the papers these days, I sometimes think he might not have been so wrong.

I remember standing outside the cottage in the hot sunshine, watching my father help a carpenter to fit a new window frame, as I told him about my younger brother's worries. Possibly this good deed was prompted by some worries of my own. "Fret you not, stripling," my father said. "I'll look in and make sure you're all right."

I'd been hoping that he might volunteer to give up the pub while Mother was away. I should have known better. I walked away from him without another word and went back to the beach. I was about twelve, I think. Maybe thirteen. I knew quite well that once my father was in the pub, he would never leave it until he was thrown out.

The first evening my mother was away, my Father came back to the house with us, and even cooked us bacon and eggs. "You can cook bacon and eggs, can't you?" he said to me. "It's easy." I didn't mind the thought of cooking for us in future. I thought it would be good to know how to feed us, since I wouldn't have bet threepence on his being around the next night. But it confirmed me in the idea that my father couldn't be relied on.

After the meal was eaten, my father fidgeted around for a while. You could see he wanted to be elsewhere. Then he said, "Put yourselves to bed, there's good lads."

I glanced towards my younger brothers. "You will look in on us later, won't you?" My real reason for saying this, though, was not brotherly concern but filial malice.

"I will, I will!" he said, and off he went.

You can imagine how dutifully we put ourselves to bed. We stayed up until 'hell-squealing hour' as my Grandmother used to say, and we made cocoa and ate all the biscuits. And played football in the house. Well, we reasoned: we'd been left in charge of ourselves, so we could do as we liked. We went to bed, finally, when we couldn't keep our eyes open or hold our heads up any longer. We were thrilled to see by the clock that it was one o' clock in the morning. We'd stayed up past midnight! We felt that was dreadfully wicked and lawless.

The stairs in this house were steep, near vertical. At the top were three bedrooms. There was no bathroom. We washed in the sink downstairs.

The landing was just a little square space, hardly room enough to stand on. Directly ahead was the biggest bedroom, my parents' obviously. To the left was a small room which I had the honour, as eldest child, of having all to myself. To the right was a slightly larger room which my brothers shared, sleeping in the same bed. We all piled up the steep stairs in the dark— there was no electric light, and we couldn't be bothered with candles— and called to each other from the separate rooms, to keep each other company as we pulled off our clothes and fell into the beds.

I think my youngest brother fell asleep almost immediately, but Jim and I went on sleepily chatting about what we might do the next day, and when we might hear from Mother. Given that it was one when we went to bed, it must have been at least half-past or even later, when we heard the street door downstairs open. I'd been speaking, but I was silent immediately. Across the landing, my brother was silent. In the dark and quiet, the sudden noise broke on us with a tremendous *crack!* The degree of fright we felt shows how completely we'd accepted that our father wouldn't keep his word— otherwise, we'd simply have thought that it was him.

Instead we lay clenched and holding our breaths as the door downstairs closed and footsteps wandered softly through the downstairs' rooms. They came back to the foot of the stairs and started climbing.

Of course, it had occurred to me by then that it was my father come to 'look in on us'; but the possibility that it was one of those roaming murderers seemed equally likely. I was stifled with fear.

The footsteps climbed the stairs to the landing. The sheet tickled my ears as I heard the door of my brothers' room creak. A pause, and then the hinges of my own door stirred. I glimpsed the dark edge of it moving. Peeping through my eyelashes, I saw the shape of a man leaning through the door: his head, his shoulders. He stayed like that for a moment, then withdrew, and his steps went back down the stairs. The street door opened and closed.

A heart's beat of silence, and then Jim's voice cried, incredulously, joyfully, "He came!" And I, too, felt warmed all over; felt relief and pleasure and something like the sensation of being cuddled. A sort of psychic cuddle, if you like. Our Father had kept his promise. In the midst of all the talk and laughter in the pub, he'd remembered us, and he'd left his friends and taken the trouble to walk up the long street in the dark, and look in on us. It was one of the best moments of my childhood. I soon fell asleep.

I remembered my happiness when I woke the next day, and I remember trying to think of a way to thank my Dad for coming to see us, but being unable. It seemed rude to mention it, somehow—it would have shown that we'd had no faith in him. But I pestered him all day, asking if I could help, until he told me to take myself off and play— "while you're young," he said.

That night, we went to bed earlier— not simply because Dad would be coming to look in on us, but because we were tired. We felt safer to go to bed too. We were alone in the house, but Dad would be coming. And he did. We heard the street door open, and the footsteps went through the house, and climbed the stairs. The door of my brothers' bedroom opened, just as before; and then mine. I saw Dad's head and shoulders looking in. Two nights running he remembered us!

It still seemed disloyal to mention our surprise and pleasure to Father, but I did tell Mother. We had an arrangement whereby I went to the pub in the early evening, just as they were opening, and stood on the bare grey boards in the hallway, breathing in the smell of beer and cigarettes, and waited for her to phone. She asked how things were, and I excitedly told her, "Father's looking in on us every night!"

She said, "Of course he is!" but I could tell by the tone of her voice that she was pleased, and more pleased still when I told her how well work was coming along on the cottage, and how capably Father was overseeing it all.

You could count on him, you see, when the chips were down. She had chosen well, after all.

I can't remember exactly how long Mother was away. At the time it seemed like a couple of years— but the summer holiday seemed to last a couple of years then. It must have been a matter of weeks. She was all smiles and hugs when she got out of the taxi, so glad to see us all again. I watched her hug Father and kiss him on both cheeks, and I thought I could see, in her manner, her new appreciation of him.

Father bought fish and chips and a bottle of the best wine he could find— I don't suppose it was very good— and we had a very merry meal in the little house, with both Mother and Father at their best— warm, and funny, and seemingly delighted to be reunited.

So when, a couple of nights later, there was a screaming row, with clocks and crockery thrown, and threats and accusations— well, I was disappointed, but also strangely relieved, as you are when the hot weather cracks into a thunderstorm.

At the time the row seemed to be about Father going to the pub and visiting a woman at the harbour, but I got the full story later. Mother had been boasting to her friends in the village about what a splendid brick Father had been during her absence. "We've had our ups and downs," she said, "but he came through this time. Every single night he looked in on those boys, every single night!"

"I thought they gave me some odd looks," she told me. Finally the pub's landlady had taken her aside. She hated having to tell my mother this, she said, but she was going to find out sooner or later, and however she found out, it was going to hurt. But she hoped to spare her at least some embarrassment. The truth was, our Father hadn't looked in on us once, whatever he'd told her.

"But the boys tell me— " Mother began. The landlady interrupted. Everybody in the pub knew, and could tell her, that our Father had never once left the pub until he was chucked out at closing time. Not once. And when he had left, he hadn't gone up the hill to the house where we were sleeping. No— he'd gone with his girlfriend to her house by the harbour. Everybody knew, she could ask anybody. They'd seen him in the pub, with her. They'd seen him leave the pub, with her. They'd seen them on their way to her house. They'd seen him leaving her house in the morning.

My mother had lived in a small village as a girl. She knew how you couldn't clear your throat without everyone knowing about it by the next morning. She knew that the landlady was telling the truth. My father came from London, with all its crowds. He had an expectation of anonymity— or perhaps he didn't care. Or wanted to be caught.

"Why did you tell me he looked in on you?" Mother asked me.

I was thinking of how Father had always been up before us, how he breezed in with a fresh loaf for breakfast, saying he'd gone for an early walk— and thinking that I should have known...

"Why did you tell me a story?" Mother asked.

I said nothing, but my brothers insisted that it was no story, that Father had looked in, that we'd heard him and seen him, but Mother threw up her hands and said, "Oh boys! I know you want to believe in him— but give it up! Lying for him won't help. He'll break your hearts like he's broken mine."

It was this— what some might call a silly incident— that finally ended my parents' marriage, not the absences and girlfriends. But that didn't become clear for a while. In the meantime, there were plenty of rows, meetings to talk things over, and more rows, notes put under doors, snubbings in the street, and more screaming rows. So occupied were they by the rows that there was a small point my parents overlooked.

My brothers and I, sitting on the cottage's garden wall, couldn't overlook it. "So, who was it came and looked in on us?" my youngest brother asked.

"Somebody in the village," I said stoutly, determined to be sensible. "Somebody who knew Father was— with her."

They nodded. "Who?" Jim asked.

I know Jim believes it was a ghost. He points out that our mother settled in that village, and lived there for more than fifty years— and yet, in all that time, no one ever admitted to being the person who'd looked in on us. No one ever said anything like, 'Oh, old So-and-So, he was a good man, he used to look in on your sons— ' They surely would have done, Jim says, if it had been someone from the village.

Our youngest brother has a complicated theory about it being some part of our Father— his soul or conscience perhaps— which had come to do its fatherly duty even while the rest of him was snuggling up to Her by the Harbour. "It was a projection," he says, "a sort of living ghost, a doppleganger."

Me? It was one of the villagers, dear. Of course it was. There are no such things as ghosts, and our Father— he didn't have a conscience.

*Author's Note on 'The Footsteps On The Stairs.'*

I have to admit that I can't remember a lot about how this story developed.

I think it owes something to one of the collection of 'true ghost stories' I often read, though which collection and which story I have completely forgotten. It's certainly not a direct retelling in any case.

It also owes something to a friend's account of an event in their childhood— but again, so much has been changed and re-arranged that it's nothing like a retelling of that.

Sometimes a story pieces itself together at the back of a writer's head, while they're not paying much attention— putting itself together from so many scraps of memory, things read, things told— that it's impossible to say where, exactly, it came from.

# MOW TOP

*Among the greens and browns of the moorland, a splash of red. A toy car, a red Porsche, its paintwork rusted and grimed. Around it, miles of bog, dense heather, bilberry. The Porsche stood on a flat grey stone by a stream.*

The corner cupboard bulged with darkness, monsters and wolves. If Tim called for his parents, the monsters would hear him and know he was there, and they would reach him first.

He strained his muscles, to hold him still. Head under the blankets, he held his breath.

A footstep, and a quake as something sat on the bed. But it was Carla, and everything dissolved in relief and pleasure. "I couldn't find you," he said. "Where have you been?"

"I'm here now."

"I was scared. I think there's a monster in the cupboard."

"There are no monsters in the cupboard. I promise you."

"I was scared though," he said.

"I know. I'll stay with you until you fall asleep." And she lay down beside him. He felt the bed shift under her, felt her body alongside his.

"Goodnight kiss!" he said.

"My breath is too strong," she said. "Go to sleep."

The next day, he couldn't find her. He wandered from room to room, but she wasn't anywhere. His father was home, and was sitting with his mother on the sofa. A stranger, a strange man, was in the armchair. The stranger looked at him and said hello, and he sidled over to his mother, who picked him up and sat him on her lap.

"Is this Tim?" the stranger said. "Hello Tim!" And then he said he'd be in touch, and left. When he'd gone, Tim asked, "Where's Carla?"

His father got up, lifted him off his mother's lap and led him into the kitchen, where he gave him ice-cream from the freezer. It was raspberry ripple, and it was nice. "But where's Carla?"

"Sssh," his father said. "Eat your ice-cream."

Carla was never around in the day any more. She came only at night, and his mother never read stories to him. Carla was better at reading stories, but he liked stories and wanted someone to read them to him, even if they weren't as good.

"Don't bother your mother," his father said. "She needs to lie down."

His father started to read him a story, but then the phone rang, and he threw down the book and ran to the phone. Then he went upstairs.

The lady from next door, Auntie Jan, came in to read him a story, but she wasn't any good. Her voice went all sharp and stiff when she was reading. He said to her, "Carla only comes at night now, and she doesn't read me stories anymore."

"Do you dream about her?" Auntie Jan asked.

He said yes, and she picked him up and put him on her lap. "When is she going to come back and take me to the park?" he asked.

Auntie Jan's eyes and mouth screwed up and she hugged him. "We must hope," she said. "We must hope."

Carla came and lay beside him in the dark. "You mustn't be frightened," she said.

"I'm not."

"Good. You mustn't be sorry or sad."

"I'm not. Will you come and take me to the park in the morning?"

"I can't. Somebody else will take you."

"They won't. They're all waiting for you to come back. Why don't you come back, Carla?"

"Tell them not to be sad," she said. "Tell them to look for me by Mow Top, if they want to find me."

Next day, at breakfast, Tim said to his father, "Carla's at Mowertup."

"What?" his father said, in the tone that warned him to be careful.

"Carla said to look for her at Mowertup."

"Eat your breakfast!" his father said.

"I don't want my breakfast. Don't like it. Why does Carla only come and see me in my bed?"

His father looked scared, and that was frightening.

"I want her to take me to the park. I want her to play with me!"

His father shouted then, loud and scary. "Can't you stop thinking of yourself?"

His mother looked up and said, "For God's sake, he's a child."

His father left the room.

A policewoman came to the house. Tim knew she was a policewoman, because of the way she was dressed. There was a policewoman in a programme he watched. She sat in the armchair and he stood in front of her, and looked at her, and she looked calmly back at him. He fetched one of his cars and showed it to her, and she said it was lovely.

So he fetched his furniture removal truck, and she said that was even nicer.

"Carla liked my Porsche," he said.

"Did she?"

29

"Yes. She said she was going to have one, only a real, big one, and she'd take me for a ride in it."

"That was nice of her."

"She comes to see me when I'm in my bed."

"Does she?" said the policewoman. She watched him push the truck on the floor for a while. "Did she come last night?"

"Yes. But she won't kiss me."

"Oh, that's a shame. I'd kiss you."

"She says her breath's too strong," Tim said.

"You should tell her to go and clean her teeth."

Tim thought about it. "I will. She lies by me 'til I go to sleep—and tells me a story sometimes."

"That's nice."

"But she won't get a book and read me one. And she won't cuddle me because she's too cold. She says she'd make me cold too."

The Policewoman said nothing, and he looked up at her. "Oh," she said, as if she'd just remembered to say something. "Have you told Mummy and Daddy about this?"

"Yes."

"And what did they say?"

Tim shrugged. "Carla says to tell them not to be sorry. She says they'll find her if they look for her. I've told them where to look for her, but they don't."

The Policewoman seemed to swallow a small pebble. "Does Carla say where they'll find her?"

"'Mowta,' she says. Mount-up. Mow Tup."

"Mow Top?"

"What does it mean?" Tim asked.

The Policewoman paused before she answered, so when she said, "I don't know, Sweetheart," Tim knew it was a lie. Then she said, "You play quietly. I have to find your Mum and Dad." She got up and left the room.

Another day a man came especially to talk to Tim. He was a very big man, but he got down on the carpet with Tim, and pushed some of his cars about. He said his name was Mark, and he smiled a lot. He said, "Tim? Can I talk to you about Carla?"

"She's my sister."

"Yes, I know. Do you remember when she lived here with you?"

"She used to take me to the park and play with me."

"Yes, but she doesn't live here any more, does she? What can you tell me about that?"

Tim stared at him.

"I wonder why isn't Carla here any more? Can you tell me?"

"She is here. But only at night."

"Carla comes at night?" Mark and Tim looked steadily at each other. "Do you think, when you see Carla at night, do you think you might be dreaming?"

Tim stared.

"What does Carla say to you when she comes at night?"

"She says not to be scared but I'm not. And not to be sorry. And to look for her at Mow Top."

"Mow Top? Why does she say to look for her there, do you think?"

"I don't know. I don't know what it is."

"It's a place. Before Carla— before— When you used to see Carla in the daytime, did she say anything about going to Mow Top?"

Tim shook his head.

"Did she ever say anything about Mow Top, do you remember?"

"We used to go to the park. There's swings."

"Great swings! I know. When you used to go to the park with Carla— do you remember? I bet you talked. Did she ever say anything about meeting anyone?"

Tim stared. "Carla said there was bears in the park."

"Did she? Bears!"

"She said that was why I mustn't go out of her sight. Because of the bears."

"I see. Did she ever say anything about meeting anyone at Mow

31

Top?"

"There's not really bears in the park. She was telling a story."

"But, Mow Top?"

Tim stared again. If Mow Top was a place, he had no idea what kind of place it was. Maybe it had a bus shelter. He'd never heard it mentioned before Carla had mentioned it, and he couldn't remember her ever speaking of it when she'd been around in the day. Certainly she'd never mentioned it at the Park, because then she told him stories and jokes, and played with him.

"Okay, Tim," Mark said, "we'll leave it there. Thanks for your help. Don't you worry. But if Carla tells you anything else, you tell your Mum and Dad, there's a good lad, so they can tell me. Promise?"

"Promise," Tim said.

Mark got up and went out into the hall. Tim heard him say to someone out there, "It's a huge area to search, and with so little to go on..."

Tim took promises seriously, and the next time he spoke to Carla, he told his parents the next morning, at breakfast. "Carla said, not to be sad about her. She said she loved you, and— "

"Tim," his father said, "be quiet."

"Don't snap at him!"

"He gives me the creeps."

"He can't— "

"Don't reward him, don't pat him on the head for coming up with these fantasies."

"Nobody has."

Tim knew they were angry. He kept his head down, kept quiet, and ate his cereal.

"He's been made to feel important— and the more he's made to feel important, the more he'll keep trotting it out!"

His mother covered her face with her hands and said, through them, "We none of us can make sense of it. He's a child— a child.

He's making sense of it in his own way. And we— we've deserted him, haven't we? We've left him to cope by himself— maybe counselling— ?"

Tim's father stood up. "I can't stand to listen to it." He went out of the room. A while after, the front door opened and closed.

When Tim had finished his breakfast, his mother picked him up and sat him on her lap. "Tim," she said, and then her breath came short and tears starting to run down her face. She screwed up her eyes, snorted, and said, "Tim, I've got to tell you... It might be... that Carla— might not come back."

"I know," Tim said. "She told me she wouldn't."

"Tim," His mother's voice died in a gasp.

"She said she'd come and see me sometimes, but she wouldn't come in the day and be with us any more." He looked up into his mother's face. "She says she's on Mow Top, and you're not to be sad, you're to forget her."

Tim's mother cried so hard that she let Tim slide from her lap to the floor. He watched her cry for a while, and then went close and tried to hug her. She sat up straight, wiped her face with her hands and said, "I'm all right, I'm all right, don't worry."

So Tim went off and found his Porsche, and pretended that he was driving it, and Carla was with him, and they were going to the seaside.

He didn't see Carla much after that. He wasn't at home a lot of the time. His mother took him to stay with his Auntie Ellie, who was nice, and bought him sweets, and comics and toys, and let him go on the ride at the supermarket.

When he did see Carla, she said the same things: 'Don't be scared, don't be sad, forget me.' So he did forget her. His family went to a new house, and he rode in the front seat of a big, real removal van, just like his toy one.

Carla didn't come at all to the new house. By the time he started school, he'd forgotten her. She was hardly ever mentioned by anyone, and when she was, it didn't rouse any particular memory in him.

But at the age of ten, looking through family photographs, he asked who the girl was.

His mother said, "That's Carla. Your sister."

"Sister? I had a sister?"

"Don't you remember? At all? You two, you used to think the world of each other. When you were little."

Tim had looked at the photo, while searching his memory, listening for the least little echoes. "What happened to her?"

"She died." His mother paused, then repeated, "She died. It was very sad."

When he was fourteen, he started to think harder about a lot of things. He was alone in the house with his mother one afternoon, when she'd just got in from work, and he said, "What happened to Carla? How did she die?"

"I suppose you have to know. But we don't know, not exactly. Probably never will now. We think she was murdered."

It was a horrible shock and, at the same time, something he'd always known: something that had sifted gently into his mind over the years, without his ever paying much attention. When it was pointed out to him so suddenly, it was like an unexpected, startling slap on the back.

"She was seventeen," his mother said. "She went out with some friends— it was the birthday of one of them. She got off the bus before them, and they saw her walk off by herself. It was dark. That was the last time anyone saw her. I remember the last time I saw her. Running out the house, all dressed up, looking beautiful. I shouted, 'Have a good time!' and she shouted, 'I will!' And slammed the door off its hinges." His mother laughed. "She never came home. We never saw her again. Nobody did. Well, except the person who murdered her. If she was murdered. Nothing was ever found. Not her body, not her bag, nothing. The Police couldn't find anybody who'd seen her, not for certain, not after she got off the bus. For a long time your father thought she'd gone off with a boy, or by herself, but— He wanted to believe that, it gave him hope, but I never believed it. She'd have told me if she'd had a boyfriend. She had no reason to go off. She was happy. And even if she had, she'd have phoned us, sent us a card, something. But she never has. It's like— it's like waiting for the next drip of the tap. For ten years."

He dreamed that he walked down long, long corridors, badly lit, painted beige, with closed doors on either side. On and on he walked, and it never changed. Beige walls, beige carpet, beige doors, closed. Then a door opened in the distance, and Carla came out, closing the door behind her. She looked at him and smiled, and crossed the corridor, opened a door, went inside, and closed it after her.

When he reached the place either he couldn't find which door it was, and stood baffled— or the door was locked— or when he opened it, there was just another long beige corridor of closed doors.

He woke remembering older dreams. For an instant he remembered, vivid as life, Carla's face.

"Mow Top," he told his mother. "I saw Carla in dreams when I was little, and she always said she was on Mow Top."

He knew where Mow Top was now. It was a stretch of moorland, humped by old mine workings, grown with scrub and thickets of hawthorn and gorse.

"I know," she said. "You gave people the creeps. They did search up there, the Police... But even with dogs and what-not, they could have searched for years and not found her. Even supposing she is up there."

Carla troubled his dreams a while, but he supposed it was a period of adjustment. As a child he hadn't understood. Now he did, and it was painful. He scanned her photograph into his laptop, and would sometimes fill the screen with her face and look at her.

When he applied for University, he dreamed of her again. He was walking through a cafe, one he knew well. A woman at a table turned and waved him over. It was Carla.

He sat opposite her. Even in the dream he knew she was dead,

35

but she seemed as real and alive as anyone he saw in waking life. "University, eh?" she said. "You going to get that Porsche then?"

He answered her but, after he woke, couldn't remember anything he'd said.

She said, "I'm on Mow Top. But you won't find me now. Don't look. Forget me." And then she stood, smiled, and walked away through the tables.

When he was accepted for University, he took his old toy Porsche, which was on the shelves in his bedroom, put it in his pocket, and caught a bus out to Mow Top. He walked for miles from the road, over some rough land, until he was out of sight of everything. He couldn't see a road or houses. Nothing but rough hillsides, tawny and green; black bog-pools, and a heavy grey sky. There on a flat stone, by the side of a marshy, spreading dark stream, he placed the toy car. And walked away and left it.

*A toy car, a Porsche, bright red but grimed by rain and wind, on a flat grey stone by a small stream.*

As a member of The Scattered Authors' Society, I've taken part in several of their annual retreats, where thirty or so writers come together to talk, eat and, mostly, laugh.

During one I signed up for a collage session, based on workshops developed by my friend Jennifer Alexander, but led, in this instance, by another friend, Katherine Roberts.

We were given heaps of magazines, and told to hold in our minds the kind of story we wanted to write, or the problem we were having with a current book.

We then had five minutes to sort through the magazines, tearing out any picture or words that caught our eye.

The next ten or fifteen minutes was spent sorting through our pile of scraps, and creating a collage from them. We weren't to think too much about it.

There was that rare thing during these gatherings of authors: a complete, absorbed silence.

At the end we held up and talked about our collages. It was fascinating to see what others had done, and hear their accounts of what their chosen images meant— but when my turn came, as so often, I couldn't think of anything much to say.

I had a headline, 'Buried In An Unmarked Grave,' a picture of moorland, and a photo of a flight of cellar steps in a derelict house. I knew those steps 'led down into the Underworld,' but that was all.

The shrewd Celia Rees said it reminded her of the 'Moors Murders'— but my mind remained blank.

I concluded that the exercise, for me, hadn't worked, although I'd enjoyed it. I threw the finished collage on my bed and went off for lunch.

An hour later, I returned to my room to pick something up, saw the collage on the bed and, as soon as I looked at it, the story 'Mow Top' leaped almost fully formed into my head. I really only had to write it down.

# THE FAMILIAR

Ros Savage was in the living room, performing a simple spell to keep her maths teacher away from school, when she heard her mother's key in the lock. She pushed one more pin through the head of the plasticine figure, and went out into the hall.

Her mother looked round a little wildly, then tumbled the armful of school-books she was carrying onto the hall table. She straightened, pushing hair out of her eyes, turned to face Ros and announced, "You're old enough now to understand about these things. I'm moving in with Mike. You can come with me if you like."

For the next hour, as she moved about the house collecting various belongings and stuffing them into suitcases and holdalls, her mother explained why she couldn't live with Ros's father any more. He was unrealistic. He still thought playing in two-bit bands in back-street pubs, for people who couldn't tell a bum note from a pizza, was going to make him famous. He'd never grown up and she was tired of waiting for him to grow up. He was so selfish. And on, and on, and on.

"I'm going," she said again, when she had all her bags by the front door. "But you can come. I want you to come."

"No," Rosa said, turning her back and walking into the living room. On the coffee table, on top of the magazines, lay the plasticine man with the pins through his head. The front door banged, and Ros picked up the plasticine man and twisted his head off.

Her dad came back at one in the morning. He'd been in Lincoln, playing. When she told him, he said, "Gone? She's gone? Why's she gone?" Then he went mad and charged round the house, kicking things and slamming doors, and saying that her mother was the selfish one, always had been, always had her hand out, couldn't understand any kind of happiness except the latest gadget or fitted bloody kitchens. Ros listened, and almost wished she'd gone with her mother. The thing that hurt most in what they said about each other was that it was all true.

Eventually her father had fallen asleep on the settee. Ros went to bed, taking the plasticine figure with her. She'd baptised it Mike while waiting for her father to come home. She hadn't decided what to do with it yet.

That had been in November. The next month was miserable. They lived on sandwiches and takeaways, while laundry and dirty crockery piled up around them. Her dad was more restless and fidgety than Rose had ever known him, unable to sit still, watch a TV programme or read a page. He found out where her mother was living, and phoned her almost every night. He'd start by trying to be reasonable, and end by yelling insults down the line. Then he'd phone Gran Savage to go over what had been said again and again. The repetition was as boring as it was painful, and Ros often felt like springing up from her chair, kicking her father hard and screaming the house down. But she didn't. Instead she found her plasticine model of Mike, cut off its legs with a kitchen knife, slashed it in half, and stabbed it until it fell apart, while tears of rage and grief splashed about it.

Mike wasn't affected at all, any more than her maths teacher had been. Either magic didn't work or she was doing something wrong. Her books on magic told her that her feelings were too overwrought and out of control. They needed to be concentrated.

40

Just before Christmas, her mother phoned. "How about spending Christmas with Mike and me?"

"No, thank you!" Ros said, and hung up.

Her mother had never made any secret of the fact that she'd left home, and her father shamelessly told everyone— almost boasting about it, Ros thought. As a result both she and her father received more Christmas presents and invitations than usual that year. People felt sorry for them. Ros cringed at the thought of going to any party and facing all those sweet smiles and polite enquiries about how she was coping. Her father must have felt the same, because he suddenly said, "For God's sake, let's go to your gran's and forget all about it."

So they loaded their presents into the car and drove over to the village where Gran Savage lived. Ros left behind her present from her mother. It was on the hall table, where it had been dumped as soon as the postman had delivered it. Leaving it there had given her a sad pain, but thinking of opening it had given her an angry one, and the angry pain had been worse.

They arrived at Gran Savage's early on Christmas Eve, and even Gran Savage, who was usually blunt and curt, had been gentler than usual, all sweet and softly spoken. The falsity had made Ros feel quite ill. She sat on the sofa, listening to all that wasn't being said, feeling angry and sad, and wishing fervently that she could change the way things were. Through the window she saw the elder tree.

A short tree, it spread its branches wide. Black branches against a grey day. She got up and crossed to the window. A tree to be wary of, she knew— a witch-tree. Judas hanged himself from an elder, and witches turned into elder trees when they needed to hide. She'd read a lot about them, and her gran had always taught her that it was dangerous to cut an elder's flowers or berries without asking its permission and thanking it. All trees were powerful magically, but there was a special, sinister power in an elder.

With a glance at her gran and father, Ros left the house and went out into the garden. It was cold, and she dragged her big cardigan around her, sniffing the air. It smelt of Christmas coming— that faint

41

tang of rotting leaves and smoke that comes with the first cold weather of autumn and grows stronger as the holiday approaches.

Ros went to the elder and leaned against one of its black branches. She was wasting her time, she thought: none of her serious magic had worked. The odd wish had come true, but her maths teachers hadn't even been mildly sick, and Mike hadn't fallen under a bus, or broken his leg, or come to any harm at all. She might just as well go back into the warm.

Then she thought of what a miserable Christmas it was going to be. Every little thing they did was going to remind them that her mother wasn't with them, but instead of lying down and crying, they were going to smile, pull another cracker, and offer each other another chocolate liqueur. They were going to smile, pull crackers and eat liqueurs until they all went mad.

Suddenly Ros took one of the elder's branches in either hand and said, "Elder, Witch-tree, help me." Saying it aloud made her feel foolish, even though there was no one to hear. So she mouthed the words. "Help me," she said silently. Her interest in magic had begun when she'd found that if she wished for something hard enough— until it hurt— the thing she wished for often came true. And silently mouthing the words she wanted to shout seemed to make them more felt.

She leaned her forehead against another of the elder's branches and wished. "I want Mum to come back. Help me, Elder. I want Mum to come back for Christmas Day. Help me. Make her come back."

Her eyes screwed tightly shut, her hands gripping the branches until she felt the muscles strain in her arms, she concentrated on her wish until her whole self dwindled into a tiny dot of determination in the darkness behind her forehead.

She concentrated so hard that when she opened her eyes, the world seemed different as if it had shifted and she was seeing it from a slightly changed angle. The colours seemed brighter and bleaker than they had a moment before, and she wasn't surprised to see another face looking into hers from the other side of the elder. It was hard to remember what things had been like before she'd closed her eyes and, or all she knew, the face might have been there all along.

It was the face of a very young man, or boy. A plain, broad face, with wide, knobby cheekbones, a rather flat nose, and eyes which, because they were so close to her own, seemed particularly vivid— a dark grey mingled with ochre, like a lichen-grown stone. His hair hung to his shoulders and, strangely on such a cold, dry day, it was sopping wet.

Feeling that he was too close, she stepped back, to see him more clearly. He wore a baggy shirt, fastened not with buttons but with lacings. It was open at the throat, showing his white, knobbly chest; and the shoulders of the shirt were darkened with water, soaked by his wet hair.

The boy's trousers were so baggy they looked almost like a skirt. They were tucked into thick stockings, and on his feet he wore big, ugly shoes with wooden soles. Slowly, it began to seem odd to Ros that he was there at all, in her gran's garden, dressed so strangely and so skimpily for a winter's day. But before she could find a polite way to say any of that, the boy spoke. He said something that sounded like, "Wha bitha doo-win?"

Ros poked her head forward, frowning. "What?"

The boy spoke insultingly slowly. "What— be— thee doin'?"

Ros folded her arms and put up her head. "This is a private garden."

"Tha be trying to work a charm," the boy said.

"You're trespassing."

The boy went behind the elder and emerged on its other side, ducking under its branches. Ros saw that he limped badly on his left leg, and felt guilty for speaking so rudely. "I be gimpy," he said, as if being lame excused him for trespassing. Rose felt unable to say anything without being unkind.

"Wheer's tha ma gone?" he said.

Ros's ear quickly became attuned to his speech. Her gran spoke

43

rather like it, and she and her father could speak like it when they chose. "How do you know about my mother?"she asked. Her gran must have been gossiping. God, nobody in her family could keep a secret!

"Tha was wishing for her back," the boy said.

Ros knew she hadn't spoken her wish aloud. Things began piecing together to make a kind of sense— the dark winter's day in the half-dead garden, the cold, the witch-tree and, standing under it, this pale boy, with his odd speech and his odder clothes.

"Why's your hair wet?" she asked.

"I was drownded."

Freezing cold air seemed to gather around Ros and press as close to her as her clothes. Drenched in cold, she stood, staring. A ghost. She was looking at a ghost. And that meant it was all true— ghosts, witchcraft, everything she'd read. Within the cold she felt flickered a warmth, a pure glee. She'd asked for help, and the elder had given it.

Clenching her fists and closing her eyes, she said again, "My mother will come back for Christmas Day."

"Tha mun say, 'Gimpy, make me mother come back for Christmas Day."

With closed eyes, clenched fists and all her will, Ros repeated the words.

"And now tha mun say, 'As I do will, so mote it be.'"

Ros opened her eyes with another little warm thrill of glee. She recognised that line from her reading. It was what witches said when they made their spells. It was very powerful. She cried out into the cold air, "As I do will, so mote it be!"

Gimpy smiled, and then he wasn't there any more. He didn't fade or vanish— it was more as if the world had been rearranged so that he'd never been there at all.

Ros went back into the house. On the way she noticed the grain in the bricks of the wall, and the subtle range of their colours, from yellow to brown. She saw the green paint bubbling on the drainpipe and flaking to show dark brown, rusting iron underneath. She saw the blackened cracks in the white paint of the back door, the rain-laid dirt over the glass. Everything had the super-clarity of a dream, while the boy under the elder tree had seemed, with his pale face and worn clothes— well— ordinary.

Inside, her gran and father were drinking tea and gossiping about some of her father's old friends. They might have seemed relaxed to someone who didn't know them, but Ros saw that her father had that same restless fidgetiness about him, and there was something strained about her gran's manner— a sense of her choosing her words carefully. Not really like her gran at all.

Ros sat down at the end of the settee, and it was then that her heart began to hammer, and she felt little shivers running through her. I've seen a ghost, she thought. Then she wondered if she had, and looked about the room, thinking: I'm seeing this. Why should I doubt what I saw in the yard with the same eyes? But what she saw had that same strange super-clarity: she saw every graduation of colour, every slight mark on the wallpaper, a loose thread hanging from a chair cover. I'll have to wait, she thought, clenching her hands on her knees. If Mum comes back on Christmas Day, then it was true.

That evening the three of them walked the few yards to the village pub. Any other year Ros would have enjoyed the blind eyes being turned to her under-age presence, and the happy noise and heat. But that year her mother wasn't with them, and she was still being plagued with heightened senses. Every tinkle and thud of music from the jukebox in the passage, every giggle, squeal and squeak from the people around her, pressed on her hearing. Her eyes were filled with light from the tinsel and foil lanterns that twisted and twinkled over the bar, and she was compelled to notice every irrelevant detail: a woman's pale blue eye-shadow, the tuft of hair on a man's poorly shaved chin, the food-stain on the front of another's pullover, the tobacco stains and chipped nail varnish on a woman's hands.

It made her head ache, and when her gran left early, to make preparations for the cooking next day, she went with her. Her father, who had fallen in with old friends, stayed behind. Ros looked back as the heavy bar doors swung shut behind them, and saw him laughing with wide-open mouth as he was teased about his pony-tail.

It was a long, quiet time after, nearly midnight, when there was a thundering on the front door as if someone was trying to punch a hole through it. Gran Savage frowned at Ros and went to answer it, with Ros following close behind.

Outside stood a neighbour, who yelled, "Come on!" before starting down the path, waving his arm for them to follow.

Still standing on the step, Gran Savage shouted, "What?"

The neighbour turned and ran back towards them, shouting, "He's been knocked down! Dave's been knocked down! Come on!"

"Oh God!" And Gran Savage ran straight out into the cold night, without stopping for her coat or even to change her slippers for shoes. Ros soon overtook her, and Gran Savage, roaring for breath, was left behind.

Dizzy on her feet from lack of breath, Ros reached the pub. The crowd outside was too preoccupied at first to notice her arrival but when she was recognised, they stuck out arm and elbows to stop her getting through. That was frightening. What was she not allowed to see? And she didn't really want to see it. She kept trying to push her way through, and calling for her dad, but truly, she didn't want to see.

"It was a car come round that corner," someone told her— she vaguely recognised the face. "Drunk, must have been. Your dad went up in the air— "

The ambulance was so long in coming and, once they were in it, so long in travelling through the dark lanes to the town and the hospital. Ros's first glimpse of her father numbed her. The white brace round his neck. The red blanket (red not to show the blood?) She kept her head turned away from him after that, her teeth gritted, her heart seeming to beat slowly and achingly against a kind of paralysis. Every cry from her father was like a physical blow. "He'll be okay, love," the ambulance man kept saying, but that was like the smiles around the Christmas dinner table. Dead on arrival, she kept thinking. Dead on arrival. Gran Savage, sealed into her own fear, sat quite apart from her.

But he had been alive on arrival, and she and her gran had to sit in the waiting room, waiting and waiting, and looking at the holly pinned above the reception desk. Even there, with the smell of disinfectant and vomit and occasional squeals of pain— even there they'd put up tinsel and were pretending to smile because it was Christmas. And her own thoughts, which she'd wanted to keep concentrated on her father, wandered about over all sorts of things. If you could hurt somebody by sticking a pin into a plasticine model of them, how could you use the model to make them better? And why was it easier to hurt people than to heal them?

Then the doctor arrived to talk about head injuries and theatre, and to say that they might as well go home. "Phone tomorrow, about nine."

"And I suppose," her gran said, "I'd better phone your mother."

Ros's belly griped. She felt sick, cold and dizzy. What had she said? I want my mother here for Christmas Day. As I do will, so mote it be.

Gran Savage padded over to the phone and made a reversed charges call to her neighbour Geoff. Then they had to wait again, until Geoff came. He drove them home, seeing them through their door with many offers of help and promises to drive them to the hospital again the next day, or whenever they needed to go. "A lovely man," Gran Savage said, once they were inside, "but I'm glad to see the back of him tonight." She went straight to her chair by the fire and sat, staring blankly in front of her. It was fully ten minutes before she said, "You got your mother's number?"

Ros's heart beat faster again. She left the room and slowly climbed the stairs, finding it hard to breathe easily. She was using the slip of paper with the number on it as a bookmark in *Practical Celtic Magic*, and once she'd pulled it from between the pages, she held it for a moment, wondering whether to pretend that she'd lost it.

She went back downstairs and gave the number to her

grandmother, then stood in the door of the living room, watching and listening as Gran sat on the phone-seat and made the call, speaking in a voice too flat and tired to be anything but calm.

"Hello? Can I talk to Linda Savage, please? Hello, Linda? Brenda. Sorry to phone you so late, but I thought I'd better tell you as soon as I could. David's been knocked down."

There was a faint squawk from the other end of the phone, which made Ros's stomach cramp, as if she was going to be sick. She turned back into the other room, unable to bear listening to her gran's voice shake, unable to bear thinking of her mother hearing the news, and perhaps not caring very much. She closed the door and moved as far from it as she could, hugging herself because she felt so cold. She turned the fire up as high as it would go, and knelt in front of it.

Her gran came back in. "She's coming as soon as she can pack a few things."

Pain spread through Ros, aching in her chest and her head. Her wish was coming true. Would her dad have to die to pay for it?

Her gran had seated herself by the fire and was once more staring in front of her at nothing in particular. She was prepared to sit there and wait, apparently, until the hospital phoned or she had to get up and let Ros's mother in. Ros went over to the window, pulled the curtain aside and pressed her face against the cold glass, so she could see beyond her own reflection. The elder tree was invisible, black in the darkness.

"Gran?" she said, after a while. "Is this house haunted?"

"Oh, for God's sake, don't start that silly talk! And come away from the window. Stop letting the heat out."

That ended that conversation. There was no possibility of bringing the talk round to the elder tree and its ghost.

It was about breakfast time that Ros's mother arrived, knocking urgently. Neither Ros nor Gran Savage had been to bed. Ros left the chair in which she'd been dozing uncomfortably and went, her face feeling white and numb, to open the door. She turned the knob and walked away, leaving her mother to push open the door herself. Ros didn't feel up to greetings.

Linda Savage marched up the hall, dumped her bulging flight bag on the living-room floor and looked round expectantly.

Gran Savage pushed herself up from her chair. "I'll make some tea. Do you want anything to eat?"

Conversation, over a breakfast of tea and toast, was stiff and formal. Linda asked for another account of the accident, and one was given, briefly. She asked what the doctors had said and was told, even more briefly. "I've got to phone at nine," Gran Savage said, pulling a face. "Christmas Day."

Ros said nothing and ate nothing. Her stomach was too unsettled for her to eat. She sat looking at her mother, at her curly, shoulder-length hair and face made up for some Christmas party. She wore jeans and a jumper, but long, shiny ear-rings still dangled from her ears. It's your fault, not mine, Ros suddenly thought, with relief and glee. I made the wish, but it was because of you I made it.

At nine, Gran Savage phoned the hospital. Ros and her mother stood near her listening in as she said, "Yes... Yes, I see... Yes, I understand...Yes, thank you." Ros wanted to snatch the phone from her.

Gran Savage put down the phone, and had some trouble keeping her voice and face under control. "He's out of theatre. They think it went well. But he hasn't come round yet, so they don't know."

"Can we go and see him?" Linda asked.

"This afternoon. But only two of us... I'll go and ask Geoff if he can take us." And Gran Savage went out of the front door without her coat.

Linda turned to her daughter. "You went yesterday, so I'm going."

Ros turned her back and walked into the living room.

Gran Savage came back to say that Geoff would take them, and then they had to wait until it was time to start out. It was a long, dreary wait, with hardly any talk. They did discuss which neighbour should come in to 'sit' with Ros while they were away, but Ros put an end to that by insisting that she would rather be alone. "Do you think

49

I'm going to play with matches?"

They lapsed into silence again, and it was a relief when Geoff knocked at the door, and Gran Savage and Linda left for the hospital.

"Look after yourself!" Linda said, and Ros's face tightened with anger. The door closed behind them. "Happy Christmas!" Ros said to the paintwork.

Alone in the silent house, Ros sat by the fire with one knee folded under her, staring blankly at a frightening future. Then, without thinking about it, she rose and went through the kitchen and out into the back garden.

The cold was sharp, but she wouldn't go back inside for a coat. Cold seemed a small thing to suffer while her father was in hospital. She stood hugging herself in the middle of the garden, not yet allowing herself to look at the elder tree. The grey December light spread over the brown fields beyond her gran's fence, and from a neighbour's house came a faint, jingly sound of music playing.

The elder tree at the edge of the lawn was thick, black and old. Its blackness seemed to make the air around it greyer and colder. "Gimpy!" she said, and hoped that she was being foolish.

He was standing by the elder tree. He had been standing there all along. The sight of his thin white shirt and his dripping hair, made Ros shiver. The wind didn't move his hair or shirt. She took a step closer and stood looking at him for a moment, then slowly reached out a hand and made herself touch him.

She expected to touch another solid human being because that's what her eyes saw. At the same time, she expected her hand to touch nothing but air, since she'd always understood that ghosts had no substance. Instead, she found her fingers sinking into something that felt like slightly warmed wallpaper-paste. She snatched her hand back, resisting the impulse to wipe it on her clothes, and held it away from her. She looked at the thing, with its dripping hair, and its loose white shirt which wouldn't flutter in the wind, and said, "My mother's come."

A smile came to his face. "As tha will, so mote it be."

"Did you make the car hit my dad?"

It still smiled. "Tha mother wouldn't come for less."

"And my dad— will he die?"

Gimpy looked at her. Water from his hair ran down his face, dribbling past his grey, stone-and-lichen eyes like tears. "My dad died."

"But will mine?"

Gimpy leaned against the elder. "My dad had eight sons. The eighth, he was the babby. The seventh, he was special. I was sixth, and gimpy."

"But will my dad die?"

"Me dad said, 'Come for a walk with me.' We was by the brook. He took me by the scruff and dowked me head under and drownded me."

Ros shut her mouth and listened.

"He copped me last breath in a bottle, and he put it back into me, and cut his own wrist and dripped blood in me mouth. He buried me under here— " His hands touched the branches of the elder tree. "He called me out when he wanted me. I haunted folk for him, and stole for him, and went under the earth for him, to ask the dead his questions."

"He was a witch, your dad," Ros said. He nodded, "He made you his familiar." She'd read about familiars— spirits attendant on, and obeying, witches.

"He died," Gimpy said. "His last breath went loose— where it blowed him, I dunno. I couldn't follow him, I baint dead. Baint alive, baint dead." He limped around the elder and emerged from under its black branches, staring at her. "I'm hungry."

"Will my dad die?"

"I care nowt for thy fairther. I'm hungry."

Ros stood silent, realising that it was asking for food. "You eat?"

"Blood." It stared at her.

"And if— I give you— ?"

"Then I'll follow thee, I'll be thine servant— and tha fairther'll

51

live."

Without hesitation, she held out her arm— but then drew back. "He'll be— well? Not crippled? Not a cabbage?"

The familiar glared at her, with its stone-grey, ochre-flecked eyes. "Dead or alive?" it asked, like the old game her father had played with her when she'd been small.

"Alive," she said, and held out her hand, the inner wrist, with its blue veins, turned uppermost. Gimpy came from the tree, took her wrist in the soft grip of both his hands, and lowered his head. She felt the bite of his teeth— sharp, yet not sharp enough to hurt— and then she felt a chill even colder than the wind, followed by a curious flush of warmth, and a little dizziness, before Gimpy raised his head. His mouth was bloodied with her blood.

"Now if my dad isn't well," she said, "I'll lay you the cruellest way I can." She found herself looking at the wintery garden, where no Gimpy had ever been.

She went indoors, where it seemed hot, so chilled was she by the wind and blood loss. She washed her wrist under the tap, wondering whether to put a plaster on it, but there was hardly anything to be seen— two small raised lumps, like flea-bites. So she didn't bother with a plaster and went into the main room, where she sat and waited in a state of blankness for the telephone to ring.

When it did, and she answered it, she head her gran's voice wobbling near to tears. "He's woken up, your dad! He isn't out of the woods yet, not by a long chalk, but they say he will be okay. Isn't that good?" Ros murmured something. "We'll stay a bit longer and then we'll be back home. Isn't it good? Don't worry!"

Ros went back into the other room and sat by the fire. After half and hour, when it was darker, she said, "Gimpy?"

Gimpy was sitting on the hearth-rug as if he'd always been there. "We've made our bargain now, haven't we?" She hadn't read all those books on witchcraft for nothing.

"Blood for service," he said.

She looked at her wrist. "What if I didn't give you any more?"

52

"I'd kill whatever tha loved."

Ros nodded. She sat in silence while the room grew darker still, and the strange thing on the hearth still sat there. She asked, "Gimpy, could you make mum stay? Alive," she added hastily, "and happy. And everyone else alive too, and happy."

Her familiar nodded.

And once that had been arranged, there'd be other things. What was a bitten wrist and a little blood lost every day? She could wear a wide bracelet. And take iron supplements. Power had to be paid for. It was worth it.

# AUTHOR'S NOTE ON 'THE FAMILIAR.'

This was originally written for a collection of scary stories by different writers.

I based it on an idea I found in Icelandic folklore. There is, in Icelandic belief, a kind of ghost called 'a follower' which attaches itself to an individual— or, often, to a family, following them down generations.

A similar belief is found in British folklore— for instance, the Banshee, or the many ghosts which announce the death of various titled families.

In Icelandic folklore, a witch or wizard can create this kind of ghost— often by murdering someone— and 'send' it against their enemies.

I used the same legend as a basis for my book, 'The Ghost Wife,' which is available as an e-book.

# ACROSS THE FIELDS

A brazier held the fire in the centre of the hut. Its iron bars were crumbling with rust, but the coals were red-hot inside, sending out waves of heat to meet the long thin draughts of cold wind that came in through the gaps in the planking walls. The men, their bodies blackened with a coating of sweat, water and coal-dust, crowded close to the fire, shivering and trying to wipe themselves dry with old rags, shirts or sheets of newspaper.

"Never mind— Christmas tomorrow!"one of them shouted, and the others laughed. Christmas Day was the only day in the whole year the mine didn't work.

When they were more or less dry, though still filthy with coal-dust, the men pulled on trousers, shirts and jackets. In 1924, there were no pit-head baths. They crowded round the fire, shoulders jostling, trying to get warm before the long, dark walk home. From hand to hand passed the jug of beer the mine-owner left in the hut for every shift of men coming up the shaft. As they drank, or waited for their turn to drink, they listened to the wind blowing around the hut and shrieking in the gaps.

"Our Grace'll be walking tonight," one of the men said, and there was more laughter.

There was a rap on the door of the hut, which only the nearest man heard. He opened it a crack, and then pulled it wide to allow someone to come in.

"Jon!" he called. "Tha little sister's here, come to walk home with thee, so tha don't get scared!"

That made all the men laugh again, and several of them began coughing badly. The girl recognised her brother's cough among them, sharp and loud. Jon almost always coughed when other people laughed.

The men crowded together to let the girl come to the fire and stand beside her brother. She was about thirteen, tall for her age, and thin, wearing a long, limp skirt that almost hid her boots. On her head was a man's old cap, with a thick tartan shawl folded over it and wrapped tightly about her body. Between the cap's peak and the shawl her eyes glistened brightly, and her nose glowed a bright red from the cold outside.

She looked quickly and shyly at all the men's faces. Even though she was standing beside him, she wasn't quite sure that she recognised her brother. All the faces were black and shining as if they'd been polished with the black lead that her mother used on the cooking-range at home: and in the tawny, golden-red light from the fire, their faces shone gilded, as the range shone by the light of the fire. But their eyes glittered white, and every glance and swivel of their eyeballs seemed exaggerated and comic and horrible all at once. And their lips, washed by the beer were bright red.

With a final cough the man beside her said, "What's up, Emily?" Then she knew it was Jon.

"Hast been paid?" she asked, and jumped as all the men around her laughed aloud.

"After thy money! Her's learning early!" one said.

"I shall be paid tonight," Jon said.

"Mother wants thee to fetch the meat for we Christmas dinner."

Jon nodded, and took the big jug from the man beside him. As he drank, the other miner asked the girl, "Tha walk here on thy own, me flower? In the dark?"

She nodded.

"And tha weren't scared?" he asked. He grinned at her, teeth white in the black mask of his face.

From the other side of the brazier, another man asked, "Didst meet Our Grace?"

"Ar, with her dead white face and her long wet hair hanging down her back," said another, "and her eyes staring, and her hands reaching out for whoever her can find— "

The miners laughed as the girl turned aside from them, pretending she wasn't interested. She knew who they were talking about: everyone in the neighbourhood knew the story of the Grace, the gypsy girl who had drowned herself in the flooded clay-pit, and now, so people said, walked over the fields at night, trying to find and drown others.

"Jon, hurry up," Emily said. "We've got to get that meat."

"Plenty of time," Jon said. It was true. The market would stay open until at least nine, and it could only be about seven now.

"Her don't want to be out late," said a miner, and nudged Jon. "If tha'm out late, tha might meet Padfoot." He stooped towards Emily. "Tha sure tha didn't hear Padfoot padding along after thee as tha come along that path?"

"I don't believe in ghosts," Emily said, and the hut was filled again with the row of the miners' laughter.

"Hey, be serious though," said another miner.

"Hast ever heard that screaming as tha was walking home?" asked a third man. "I remember the time—"

Emily moved close to Jon and looked pleadingly up at him. She didn't want to hear any more of these frightening stories. Jon smiled his red lipped smiled and shouted, "Happy Christmas, lads! We'm going."

He reached out and opened the door of the hut, letting in a broad, cold blast of air as he and Emily moved out into the darkness, followed by a cheery, beery chorus of, "Happy Christmas! Happy Christmas, little un! Happy Christmas!"

57

Outside in the dark, another fire burned near the mine-shaft, an open, brick-lined hole in the ground. It was the only light to be seen nearby; beyond its flickering was deep darkness. Jon passed by the fire with his quick, long stride, and Emily hurried after him, her boots clop-clopping on the stony, hard-frozen ground. Above them glittered a wide expanse of silver stars.

A black shape loomed up ahead— the mine office. They rounded the building, and Emily was glad to see yellow lamplight spilling from its windows. She waited outside, leaning against the wooden wall and hugging herself inside her shawl, while Jon went in to hand over his candle-can and collect his money. Emily was cold and wished he would hurry up. Even there, in the mine yard, she didn't like the dark. She couldn't help thinking that Our Grace might suddenly whip into sight, with her long wet hair, her white drowned face and her reaching hands.

Even the knowledge that Jon and the light of the mine office were only a step behind her didn't make her feel any better. She would still have seen Grace— her swollen drowned face and her mouth moving as she called your name.

Quickly Emily pushed the door and went into the office, to stand close behind Jon, so close that she touched him. Being near her brother always made her feel better. He never seemed to be afraid of anything: not of going underground, nor of the dark, or big dogs, or strangers, or mice, or spiders or anything. Yet still she looked fearfully towards the door, wondering if the yellow light of the oil lamp would really keep Grace out of the office if she were in the yard.

Jon felt her touch against him, looked down and smiled. "Come on, Chuck," he said, moving towards the door. She followed him. It meant going out into the dark again, but at least now she would be with Jon, and she didn't fear ghosts as much while he was with her. He walked to work in the dark most days, he worked all day in the dark and walked home again in the dark, and he thought nothing of it. Ghosts didn't come near people who didn't believe in them, did they? So Emily hoped.

Jon had worked hard all day, but he still walked fast as he led the way, by dark, unlit field-paths, towards the town of Oldbury and its market. Emily had to put many a hop and skip in her walk to stop herself from falling behind. Slipping one hand out of her shawl, she gripped him by the belt to help herself.

"Here," he said. "Keep thy hand warm." And he slipped her arm through his, and held her hand in his dirty warm one. His hands were always hot, as if he had a fire burning in him. But she was still out of breath by the time they reached Oldbury.

The market place was lit by flaring white gas lamps with pitch-black shadows between pools of light. There were still many people about: all those who had delayed shopping for their Christmas dinner as long as possible in order to buy cheap. Jon and Emily kept their arms linked as they pushed through the crowds and made their way to the butcher's stalls, where blood had collected in pools between the cobbles, and where chickens' heads and legs lay scattered everywhere. Even in the cold, there was a bad smell of blood and flesh and chicken guts.

Jon was tired and wanted to get home, bath and sleep, so he didn't take long about marketing. On one stall he spotted a large goose hanging by its legs.

"I bet," he said to Emily, "that he can't sell that. Too big. Nobody wants it. How much for the big 'un, mate?" he called to the stallholder, pointing to the goose.

The stallholder looked up at the bird and pulled a face. He knew that he wasn't going to sell the bird, and he had no way of keeping it fresh to sell another day. "Seven and six," he said.

"I'll give thee five shilling," Jon said, and the stallholder took the bird down without another word and began wrapping it in newspaper.

Emily wasn't happy. "Too much!"she whispered.

"It's Christmas," Jon said, and went on to buy sweets for her and for the two other sisters and three brothers at home.

"We'll have no money left," Emily said, wanting the sweets, but afraid of what their mother would say.

"It's my money," said Jon.

They started walking home, Jon's pockets stuffed with bags of sweets, and his arms wrapped round the goose. Emily held on to his belt to help her keep up, her hand warmed by the shelter of his jacket and the heat of his body through his shirt. She was tired, having been up early to scrub the kitchen floor before going to school, then running errands after school and finally coming on this long walk with her brother. She leaned her head on his arm as they walked.

Once they were out of town, they were faced with a long, long road home. Jon suddenly stopped walking, hugging the goose to himself and lowering his head. Emily knew that he was overcome with the thought of how far they had yet to walk before they were home. And then he still had to bath before he could go to bed. "It'd be shorter," he said, "if we cut across the fields."

Emily straightened up, lifting her head from his arm. She didn't like the idea at all. The fields were wide, cold, empty and dark. But she had to give a more sensible reason than that. "It's dangerous," she said. "What about all the old pit-workings and quarries? We might fall in one."

"I'm not walking all the way round," Jon said, turning off the road and striking out across the rough ground of the field.

Emily let go of his belt and stood for a moment. She thought about walking home by herself. She looked about, up and down the road, but there was no one in sight, and the roadway, lit only by widely spaced gas lamps, seemed darker without Jon. And Jon, with his quick, long stride, and without her hanging on his belt, was already growing smaller, fading into the darkness. Even walking across the fields, she decided quickly, was better than walking all that way by herself, thinking about drowned Grace, and the ghost dog, Padfoot, whom you saw when you were going to die.

"Wait for me, Jon!" Hugging her shawl about her, Emily ran from the road over the field. The frozen ground was just as hard underfoot as the pavement, and frozen leaves rustled under her boots. Jon stopped and turned, waiting for her. Breathless, she caught up with him and wrapped her fingers about his belt again, under his jacket.

"We'll soon be home," he said. "Have a mince pie afore we go to bed."

They didn't waste much breath on talking after that. Emily was surprised, as always, that Jon could walk so quickly after spending all day crouching underground hacking at rock and coal. He swung on, stride after quick stride, hugging the dead goose to his chest, his head lowered to watch where he put his feet, his breath drifting before in puff after puff of white mist. Emily's own breath wreathed her face as she painted beside him, forced to work her legs just a little too fast, so that her hips ached. Her heels jolted hard on the ground and shook her with every step. Her throat was raw from gasping at the freezing air, but she didn't ask Jon to slow down. After all, she thought, peering round them into the dark, the quicker they walked, the sooner they would be home, and safe from the night.

The fields around them could only be felt as a cold open space, over which the wind blew to scrape at them. Nothing could be seen but blackness; even the path beneath their feet was only a dimmer grey in the darkness. Emily hoped they were on the right path: in the dark, it could be any path. And anything could be out there, in the darkness, hidden from them.

As they walked, Emily kept looking all round, glancing back over her shoulder every few seconds, and squinting her eyes to peer into the darkness ahead. If there was any danger, she wanted to see it before it reached them. But despite this care, she didn't see the man coming. She only heard his voice, suddenly barking out in the darkness on Jon's other side: "Evening."

Emily leaned around Jon and saw a stranger walking beside her brother. In the dark, she could just make out the darker area of his working clothes and the pale white stripe of his muffler. Between the muffler and the dark cap was the not-so-pale blur of his face.

"Evening," Jon said, friendly and unafraid, while Emily clung more tightly to his belt and pressed closer to him. The man was not the ghost she had feared, but now she was afraid that he was a robber or a murderer, who'd been waiting for them on this dark field path. "Happy Christmas," her brother added.

"Oh," said the man, his deep voice grumbling through the dark, cold air. "It aint Christmas yet. Not 'til the last stroke of midnight."

Their feet crunched on the frost hardened path— Jon's light, quick, steady tread and Emily's skip, hop and jump. She listened, but the stranger's feet made no sound.

The stranger spoke again. "Where thee going?"

"Home," Jon said. "As quick as we can."

"What's thy hurry?" asked the stranger. "Why don't tha come to the match? Tha could win a prize, strong lad like thee."

"Match?" Jon asked, and Emily tugged at his belt and whispered, "Jon!" But he either didn't hear or took no notice.

"Wrestling match," said the stranger. "I know thee for a good wrestler, lad."

"Jon, we've got to get home," Emily said.

"There's prizes?" Jon asked. Their family always needed money or extra food, especially at Christmas. Whether the prize was money or a cake or another goose, it tempted Jon.

"There's prizes," said the stranger, and Emily didn't like the way he said it— as if there were other things he wasn't saying.

"A bout or two then," Jon said, not seeming to notice anything odd about the way the man had spoken. Emily tugged at his belt but he ignored her, and she could have wept with anger and disappointment. She so much wanted to get home and safely into the warmth and light.

"Oh Jon, let's go home," she wailed. "Tha'm tired. Come home, go to bed."

Jon looked round. "Thee run on home," he said, sounding bad tempered.

Emily looked ahead at the thin path of hard dirt that ran through long, grey tussocks of wilted, frozen grass and leafless bushes, and quickly faded into black winter darkness. She almost did as he said: she could see herself, in her imagination, running hard along the path until she reached the safety of streets and houses. In imagination, she could feel her running feet hitting the ground.

But she was afraid of what she might meet on her own, without Jon's warmth and confidence to keep the ghosts away. And she was afraid to leave her brother alone too, without her fears to warn him, trusting and friendly as he was. As he protected her, so, she felt, she protected him: they should stay together. Who knew who this stranger was, or what he really wanted? He might kill Jon to get the goose.

"I'll come with thee," she said, in a small, frightened voice.

She imagined the man taking something heavy from his pocket, like a brick or an iron bar, and hitting Jon on the head with it, and she knew she couldn't stop him, but she also felt, fiercely, that she could try. She could kick the man hard; she could bite him till he bled. She could shout and shout, louder than she'd ever shouted; she could run and fetch help. Even if she couldn't stop the man hurting Jon, she could make sure he didn't get away with it.

The stranger left the path and struck off through the long, crunching, frozen grass of the field. Jon followed him and Emily, clutching at Jon's belt, followed Jon. Whenever she could, Emily peered around Jon at the stranger, trying to see what he looked like so that she could describe him to the police if she had to. But she could never see his face clearly. It was always hidden by his cap, or by his turned up collar and muffler. She thought he had a dark moustache; she thought his cheeks and chin were darkened by beard stubble, but that was as much as she could tell.

Just you try anything, she thought at him. Just you try. I'll kick your feet from under you. I'll bite your fingers off. I'll— she wished very much that she was bigger and stronger.

They were very far from the path now, and when Emily looked around and behind them, she saw nothing but deep, blue-grey darkness, with black shapes of low bushes emerging from it. But from a head came a noise. It was a murmur, buzzing and rising and falling: the sound of voices clamouring together as they had clamoured in the market-place— but here the sound had a colder, more frozen note as it faded and was lost in the open fields. She wanted to ask Jon, one more time, not to go to this meeting, but to come home with her— but she knew that he wouldn't change his mind now.

There was a light ahead: red and golden light, shining out of the darkness like a jewel. Black shapes moved across it, blocking out its light and letting it shine again— a fire with people moving around it. Jon picked up his heels and walked even more quickly, to reach the fire and the people, and Emily had to run to stay with him. She felt tears in her eyes as she ran towards what frightened her.

They came nearer to the fire, and felt its heat blow towards them on the wind, bringing a shower of sparks and cinders together with an ashy smell of burning. The stranger began to clap his hands and shout, "Here we be, here we be! Here's a lad to give us a bout! Here's a lad who'll bet his wages, his goose and his heart and soul!"

Emily didn't like the sound of that; and she didn't like it when the people left the fire and came to meet them, crowding around them so that they were hemmed in. She didn't like it when men pressed close and began to slap Jon on the shoulders, because she was so small among them that she felt she was being smothered in the crowd, and because she was afraid she would lose her grip on Jon's belt and be pushed away from him. She took hold of his belt with both hands, and let herself be dragged almost off her feet as he was carried forward in the noise of the crowd, closer to the light and heat of the fire.

A dark young man, as tall as Jon but broader, stood squarely between them and the fire. His face was in deep shadow and couldn't be seen. He started to take off his jacket, and as he did so, he said, "For the goose."

Jon grinned and passed the goose to Emily. She took it, soft, limp and heavy, in her arms. Jon took off his cap and put it on Emily's head, on top of the shawl and cap she already wore. He unwound his muffler and hung it around her neck; and he took off his jacket and draped it around her shoulders. Then, in his shirt-sleeves, in the bitter cold, he bent at the knees and held his arms out to the other young man. The crowd around them backed away to give them room.

Emily hated being there and having to watch. She felt desperately that Jon must win— felt it so much that it hurt— not only because he was her brother but because if he lost the goose, the whole family would have to go without Christmas dinner, and the five shillings spent on it would be wasted. She didn't think they would dare go home and face her mother after spreading five shillings on a goose and then losing it.

And wrestling was a rough game. The other man looked heavier than Jon. If he was a better wrestler as well, then Jon could be badly hurt, and if Jon was hurt, then he wouldn't be able to work, and they were always short of money even when Jon was in work. Jon had to win, he had to, he had to! She hugged the goose tightly, and swallowed over a painful, hot lump in her throat.

The two men wrapped their arms around each other, and were now trying to crush the breath from each other's ribs, while struggling to trip each other with their feet. Emily watched, her unblinking eyes watering in the cold, wishing hard for Jon to win. But the fear that he would lose was equal to all her hope. It was unbearable— unbearable to hope and fear so much, and she had to turn away from the wrestlers.

She found herself looking instead at the faces in the crowd, lit warmly red and gold of the firelight. And her eyes picked out one woman's face. She had seen that woman somewhere before—

She jumped as a shout went up all around her, shaking the cold air. Jon was on the ground. The other had thrown him down. As she watched her brother got up and again the two men wrapped their arms around each other.

Emily looked again for the woman in the crowd. She couldn't see her any more, but she noticed a man. She knew his face too, but couldn't think of his name...

There was another shout, and Jon was on the ground again. Jon was losing! Oh, Jon! she thought, hugging their goose, their Christmas dinner, which others were going to eat: how could tha win when tha was so tired? Why didn't tha come home with me?

She had to look away again. And there was another face she knew: the face of a boy this time. Now she knew that boy's face very well. Who was he...?

The crowd shouted a third time, but Emily didn't look to see which of the wrestlers had been thrown. She remembered where she had seen the boy before. He had been in her class at school— had it been last year or the year before? But he was no longer at school because— she turned even colder as she remembered— because he had died, of consumption. She had seen his funeral go past in the street, and everyone had stopped, taken off their hats and bowed their heads. They had prayed for him at school, and had been asked to remember him. Dead and buried, that boy, yet here he was at this Christmas Eve wrestling match, out in the wild, dark fields.

She felt a tugging at the goose in her arms, and looked up into the face of the dark young man, Jon's opponent. He was taking the goose from her. "I won," he said. And he wasn't even out of breath.

Emily let him take the goose, because he had won it and because she was afraid. She remembered where she had seen the woman she had noticed earlier... That woman had lived three doors away from them when Emily had been a little girl, until she had gone away. It had been a long time before Emily discovered that the woman had died. And the man she had noticed... She had seen the man with Jon. Long ago, when Jon had first started working down the pit, he had worked with that man. Emily had seen them outside the pub, laughing and joking together. And Jon had gone to his funeral after he had been killed by a roof-fall in the mine.

Shrinking in on herself, hugging herself small, she glanced quickly at the crowd about her, and thought: Dead, all dead. We're in company with the dead.

Jon had got to his feet, and had come over to her, and the young man who now held the goose.

"I wasn't ready," he said, breathing hard and short out of breath. He coughed before adding, "Again. I'll win the goose back."

"Jon," Emily said, reaching out for him. "No." She wanted to tell him about the people around them. She wanted to point out the dead neighbour-woman and his dead workmate and her dead school friend. But her voice squeaked like a mouse, and Jon took no notice of his nervous little sister.

"The goose if tha win," said the dark, dead young man. "What if I win?"

Jon reached into his trouser pocket and they heard the jingle of coins.

"I've no use for money," said the dark young man.

Jon dropped the coins back into his pocket and looked up in surprise. "What, then?"

Emily felt all the people— all the dead people— move closer; and she darted to Jon and put her arms around his waist. He absent-mindedly dropped his arms around her shoulders as he waited for an answer.

"Thy heart and soul," said the dark young man.

Emily hugged Jon tighter in warning, but Jon laughed and coughed, and said, "Me heart and soul? What use be them to thee?"

The fire flared and its red light glowed over the dark young man's face, showing the damp twist of his hair and the deep hollows above and below his eyes, the skin stretched tight over his cheekbones, and the shape of his teeth showing through his lips.

As Emily held onto Jon, she felt him start with shock. "Tom Rugeley!" he cried, drawing a long breath of cold air, which made him cough. Emily, hugging him, felt the coughs shake him. "Tha'm dead, Tom," Jon said. And then he said, to himself, "I'm dreaming."

"Bet me thy heart and soul," said Tom Rugeley. "I'll dance to the beat of thy heart— mine don't dance no more. I'll feel with thy soul— mine don't feel no more. If I win, I'll live in thee— and thee won't live no more."

Emily felt Jon's arm tighten round her, and his other arm come round her too. He lifted her right off her feet, up to his chest, and she felt him move a step or two. He was going to run and take her with him. But then he stopped, and looking about, Emily saw the people all around them, coming closer, their arms held out to block their way. Jon's grip on her loosened, and she slipped back to the ground. There were too many of the dead, all around them, and all too strong. They could not run away.

"Then we'll wrestle," Jon said, "but here's the wager. If I lose, me heart and soul. But if I win, the little wench goes home with the goose."

When she heard that, Emily's heart swelled and grew full and sore with love and gratitude. Tears pressed against the backs of her eyelids, and she took Jon's warm hand in both of hers and held it tight.

All around them the dead murmured and whispered, and to the front of the crowd came pushing the dead women, the young girls, and the little girls who had died as children. They all stared at Emily with their sunken eyes and there was one— Emily shivered and hid her face against Jon's shirt sleeve— there was one with long black hair hanging over her shoulders that dripped water on to the ground even in this freezing weather. The whispering, the murmuring from all the dead women and girls said, "But we want her. We want her…"

"Then it's a good wager!" Jon said. "More to win, more to lose! My heart and soul against the little wench and the goose. What tha say, Tom?"

Tom Rugeley looked around at the dead, and then he looked back at Jon and slowly, despite the cold whispering in the air, he nodded.

Jon pushed Emily gently away from him and the second wrestling match began.

Emily watched this time, gritting her teeth until her jaws ached as Jon strained to throw the dead man and not be thrown himself. By sheer skill, he got his foot around the foot of the dead man, and threw him over his hip to the ground. But the dead man got up again at once— no struggle can tire nor fall hurt a dead man— and closed with Jon again. And Emily watched, her heart aching more each time as her brother was thrown once, twice, three times, and lost the match.

How else could it have ended? Jon had worked all day, and walked to market and back, and fought one bout already, while his opponent would fight always with the same untiring strength. Jon had lost, and now he lay on the hard, frozen ground where he had been thrown, while all the dead turned to Emily.

"New lives for old," said Tom Rugeley. "Who shall I give the little wench to?"

"Thou hasn't won me!" Emily said. Her voice shrilled out through the dark, sharp with fright. "Jon lost, so tha've won him, heart and soul. But tha've not won me."

"Art going to wrestle?" asked Tom Rugeley, and around them came the dry laughter of the dead.

Emily ran across the little open space at the centre of the gathering, to where Jon half sat, half lay, on the ground. She took his jacket from around her own shoulders, and put it around his. "I can't wrestle," she said, "but I can riddle. I'll ask thee a riddle. If tha can answer it, tha shall ask me one. First one who can't answer loses."

"But what's the wager?" asked the dead man.

"If I lose, tha wins us both," said Emily. "If I win, tha loses us both. And the goose."

"Win all, lose all," Tom Rugeley said.

The dead crowded close; the dead whispered and shook their heads. But Emily said, "Fancy a dead man being scared to take a bet!"

"You're on!" said Tom Rugeley.

"And I'll ask the first riddle," she said. And she asked the hardest one she knew— one she'd learned at school.

*"In a hall as white as milk,*

*Lined with skin as soft as silk,*
*In a fountain crystal clear,*
*A golden apple does appear.*
*No doors there are to this stronghold,*
*Yet thieves break in and steal the gold.'*

What is it?"

"That's an old one," said Tom Rugeley, "and the answer's known to all of us here. It's an egg. And now I ask one. How many wild strawberries grow in the salt sea?"

Emily, kneeling on the ground beside Jon, looked into his face, hoping he might know the answer, but it was plain he had no more idea than she had. "How many wild strawberries...?" she repeated, and knew that the answer must be a tricky one.

And then it seemed to her that she'd heard the riddle before, and knew the answer. She snatched at it without wondering what it meant — "As many fish swim in the forest!" The shoulders of the dead people around them sagged in disappointment.

"Here's my next riddle." It was another she'd learned at school.

*"White bird featherless*
*Flew from Paradise,*
*Landed on the stony wall.*
*Along came Sir Landless*
*Took her up handless*
*Rode away horseless*
*To the King's high hall.'*

What is it?"

"Another old one," said Tom Rugeley. "What's old, we know. The answer's, 'a snowflake in the wind.' Here's my riddle: How quick can you travel round the world?"

This was hard. The dead man knew far more riddles than Emily did. She had no idea how long it would take to travel even to Birmingham. Then the answer jumped into her head. "One day! If you get up with sun, and keep up with the sun, you can travel round the world in one day, like the Sun. And here's my riddle."

She thought: I'd better make it a good one. A new one, because I

70

might not be able to answer another one of his, and the dead know all the old riddles. She thought frantically, while the ghosts waited. Hurry, hurry! She told herself. Think of the answer first, then make a riddle fit it. Her thoughts scurried so quickly that when she spoke the beginning of the riddle, she had no idea how it would end.

*"My heart is still, but still it longs,*
*I nothing fear but morn's bird-song,*
*By day unseen, by night showing clear—*
*Now riddle-me-ree–ah*

What be I?"

Tom Rugeley didn't answer. He stared at her, and then looked round at the other dead. "A new riddle," he said.

"If tha can't answer it," Emily said, "tha've lost."

"I can answer it, I can answer... 'By day unseen, by night showing clear...'"

Emily and Jon sat together on the cold, hard ground, and looked at each other, and waited. All around them, the dead whispered.

"It's the moon!" said Tom Rugeley.

"No."

"Then it's the stars," said a dead woman.

"No," Emily said. "Dost give up?"

"We'll answer it, we'll answer— "

The night drew on, and was colder, and colder. Emily and Jon sat wrapped in her thick, heavy shawl, huddling close together to keep warm amidst the cold company of the dead.

"I nothing fear but morning bird song," said Grace, the drowned girl, her hair never ceasing to drip. "Is it a worm?"

"No." Emily was so tired she couldn't hold up her head's weight, and leaned it on Jon's shoulder.

"'My heart is still, but still it longs,'" said the dead man who had led them there. "I can't make owt of that."

"It's a stupid riddle!" said Tom Rugeley.

"Dost give up, then?" Emily asked.

"No!" And on and on went the guessing game, until midnight

71

passed, and there came the coldest, darkest time of the night, when Emily and Jon shivered together despite the shawl, and the deep cold set Jon coughing again.

The dead couldn't guess the answer to the riddle, but they wouldn't give up their chance of winning living hearts and souls either.

"It must be the moon! It can only be the moon!"

"No," Emily said, her eyes closed.

"Then it's the stars— has to be!"

"No."

"'My heart is still...' It must be something dead," said one of the ghosts, and Emily opened her eyes and held her breath. But the right answer didn't come.

The ghosts tried, and argued, and tried again until the sky was grey, and the air still colder than it had been all night. They went on trying until, from far over the field, came the first morning cock-call, the first cock-crow of Christmas Day. And on Christmas Day, and all through the twelve days of Christmas, ghosts and the dead and witches have no power.

As the cock crowed a second time, a rustle of movement ran through the crowd of dead. They drew back from Jon and Emily and looked at each other. And as the cock crowed a third time, they turned and ran away across the dark field. Without a sound they went: no shouting, and no sound of feet on the ground. They vanished into the deep grey of the morning twilight, running for their graves in all the little churchyards round about.

Jon and Emily knelt up on the hard, cold ground, and watched them go. Jon put his arm round Emily and hugged her. They got to their feet, very slowly and stiffly, because they were so cold. Jon picked up the goose and checked that his pockets were still full of sweets, and then they went on across the field to home.

They lived in a little house that was one in a long row. Jon lifted the latch and they went in. Their whole family was gathered in the small room. Mince pies were being made at the table. One sister was rolling out the pastry; a little brother was cutting out the pies with an upturned cup; another was greasing tins. Their mother was putting mincemeat into the cases. Everyone stopped and looked up as the door opened.

"Where hast been?" their mother shouted.

"We come across the field and we got lost," Jon said.

"I thought the bogey-man had got thee," said their mother.

Jon and Emily looked at each other, and Jon handed the goose to their mother.

"All of thee— upstairs!" said their mother to the children. "Jon's got to have bath. There's hot water in the copper, Jon."

All the children left the mince pies and went through to the stairs. Emily followed them, and after her came Jon, on his way to get the tin bath from the yard. At the foot of the stairs he stopped her, and whispered, "Is the answer, 'a ghost'?"

Emily grinned, nodded, and went on up the stairs.

"If you want to hide something," Jon said, "put it in full view." And he went on to fetch the bath.

Afterwards, they had roast goose for Christmas dinner, and mince pies, and when Jon walked to work in the dark, early the next morning, he didn't go across the fields, even though the twelve days of Christmas still had eleven days to run.

# AUTHOR'S NOTE ON 'ACROSS THE FIELDS.''

This was also written for an anthology of scary Christmas stories.

The story is based on an old Cornish legend I read years ago, as a child holidaying in Cornwall. In that story, it's a couple of tin-miners who are forced to wrestle evil spirits out on the moors.

I changed the setting to my own Black Country, and based it, in part, on family stories of my grandfather, who lived with his parents and many brothers and sisters, in a cottage.

The account of the miners coming up from the shaft and huddling round the brazier is based on fact, as is the description of buying late in the market, to get cheap food.

The riddle contest is common in folklore.

# THE QUEEN OF HEAVEN

# VISITS THE QUEEN OF DARKNESS

Inanna set Her mind on The Great Below. She would abandon Heaven, abandon Earth, and descend Beneath.

She called her servant Cara, to dress and adorn Her. She sat in Her gilded chair, and he took Her long, dark hair and pinned it close to Her head. He reddened Her mouth, and he painted Her beautiful eyes.

Cara said, "Will Her Ladyship join Her lord, Dumuzi in the garden?"

"That shepherd boy?"Inanna said.

"You made him Your lord, Lady," Cara said. "Such a handsome young man..."

Inanna tapped Her golden earrings, so they swung and shone. "He stinks still of sheep."

"Such a pleasant young man I have always found him," said Cara.

"I shall turn him into a wolf. It would be funny to see the other shepherds hunt him down and kill him."

"I pray Your Ladyship will not," Cara said. "Forgive me, but it was not amusing to turn the gardener into a toad."

"Oh, it was." Inanna slipped gold rings on Her fingers. "I still see him, sometimes, among the flowers. I poke him with sticks."

"Your Ladyship's sense of humour does not please everyone. Not one thought it funny when You turned the fisherman into a fish, the farmer into a weed— "

"They should not have bored Me," Inanna said.

"— the cook into a cauldron, the— "

Inanna stood, and Cara shrank back. "Little man, don't nag. I promise you, I shan't turn Dumuzi into a wolf. Yet. And today... Today, My mind is set on the Great Below. I shall visit My sister, Erishkegal." When Cara said nothing, she turned Her dark and beautiful eyes on him. "Nothing to say, Cara?"

"Lady! If You go to the Dark Land— if You enter The House of the Dead— You will never be able to return."

"I shall come and go as I please. I always do."

"But think, Lady— will Your sister welcome You?"

"Oh, The Queen of Darkness will welcome The Queen of Heaven, don't you think?"

"Eriskegal hates You, Lady," Cara said. "She hates all of us, who live in the light and air."

"You speak ill of My sister, naughty man. My mind is set. I shall take a little of the light and brightness of the world above down there into the darkness! She will love Me for it!"

"Oh, Lady— !" said Cara fearfully.

"Enough! Dress Me!"

"But Lady, truly— "

Inanna snapped her fingers, her golden bracelets clashing.

Cara brought Her things, and She chose a dress of fine, pleated linen.

Her wig, of black, oiled curls, decorated with jewelled, golden combs, was set on Her head.

A pectoral of gold, set with gems, was set on Her breast.

A necklace of gold and lapis-lazuli— the lapis bluer than the sky— was hung around Her neck.

Finally, She took in Her hand a wand, most precious, carved from lapis, and set about with leaves, flowers and bees of gold. Into all these things— dress and headdress, necklace, pectoral and wand— were woven and hammered Divine Powers.

She looked at Herself in the bronze mirror. Her skin was golden, Her eyes large, dark and brilliant, Her lips red. She glittered and glimmered with scented oil, with gold, with gems.

Cara said, "Oh Lady! You are beautiful— You are terrifying!"

"So I am," She said, and walked away.

Her minister, Ninshkurbur, rose and hurried after Her.

"Listen to Me," said Inanna to Ninshkurbur. "These are your orders. Do not neglect them! I shall, this day, go beneath, to the Underworld. If, after three days I have not returned, you must go to the ruins and there lament for Me, as you would for the dead. Go to all the God-Houses for My sake. Beat a drum in the temples' sanctuaries."

"Lady, I will," said Ninshkurbur.

"Do what you would do for the dead— cut yourself above your eyes for Me, cut your nose, cut your ears, and bleed. Dress yourself in one garment, like the poor. Make yourself dirty for Me. And go, alone, to the God-house of Enlil."

"I will do all You say, Lady."

"Lament before Enlil, saying, 'Oh, Father Enlil, don't let Your Daughter, young Lady Inanna, be killed in the Land of Darkness. Don't let Your precious metal be mixed with dirt in the Underworld. Don't let Your lapis-lazuli, that precious gemstone, be split beside common builder's stone. Don't let Your sweet scented box-wood be chopped up with rough carpenter's wood. Don't let young Lady Inanna be killed in the Underworld.' That is what you must say.

"But if Enlil will not help, go to the God-House of Nanna, and there say the same. If Nanna will not help, go to the God-House of Enki, and lament to Him. This you must do, to save Me."

"Lady, I vow I shall," said Ninshkurbur.

"Goodbye to you, then, Ninshkurbur. Do not forget My orders." And Inanna went on Her way to the Land of Darkness, taking the steep path that led beneath, to Her sister's world. The air darkened and chilled. Her feet kicked up grey dust. All the Underworld is grey dust. No rain ever falls there. Nothing grows. No birds sing.

Inanna came to the great gates of Her sister's palace. They were wide and high, banded with bronze. They were closed against Her.

Angrily, She banged on the gates. Angrily, She shouted. "Open up, doorman!"

From behind the gates, the doorman called, "Who is there?"

"Inanna, Queen of Heaven, stands here. Open up!"

"What do You do here?"the doorman asked. "Why have You set Your feet on the road which no traveller ever walks twice?"

"I wish to visit My sister."

"You have no business here. This Land is for the dead, and You are living. Go away."

Inanna cried, "Open these gates to Me, or I will smash the gateposts, I will unhinge the gates! I will set the worlds in disorder— I will let loose the dead and lead them to the upper world to eat the living!"

"Stay here and wait," said the doorman. "I will speak to my Mistress, Your sister, and tell Her You are here."

The doorman went into the palace of his mistress, the Queen of Darkness, Erishkegal. He said to Her, "Lady, Your sister Inanna is outside Your gates, demanding entrance. She has banged on Your gates, She has shouted angrily for the gates to be opened. What shall I do, Lady?"

Erishkegal sat enthroned in Her dark hall, where the grey dust had drifted in the corners and against the walls. Her tables were dusty too, for the plates were filled with dry clay, the food of the dead. When She heard the doorman's words, She bit Her lip. She hated Her sister, and did not wish to see Her, but She knew that Inanna would carry out Her threats. Erishkegal did not want Her gates thrown down, nor Her dead released.

"Send for My counsellors," She said, "and then let My sister in. But tell Her that She must follow My customs. At each of My gates

78

She must take off some jewel or garment. She must come into My presence without Her jewels, without Her dress, as the dead do. We shall strip Her of Her Divine Powers."

The Gatekeeper hurried back to the gate. Inanna stood on its other side. "Your gracious Sister says You may enter," he said, "but You must follow our custom. At every gate You must give up a jewel or garment."

"Open the gate," said Inanna.

The Gatekeeper drew back the heavy gates, and held out his hand. "Give me the wand."

"Why?"

"These are the customs and rites of the Underworld," said the doorkeeper. "Don't open Your mouth against them, Inanna. Hand over the wand."

Inanna gave him Her wand of lapis-lazuli, and so lost one of Her Divine Powers. She followed him between the dark, cold walls, through the grey dust and silence, to the second gate.

"Now give me Your wig," said the doorkeeper. "Do not open Your mouth against our rites and customs."

She took off her heavy wig with its golden ornaments, and so lost another of Her Divine Powers.

At the third gate, the gatekeeper demanded her pectoral.

At the fourth gate, She took off Her necklace of gold and lapis.

At the fifth gate She took off Her rings.

At the sixth gate, She took off her sandals.

At the seventh gate, She shed her linen dress, and so lost the last of Her Divine Powers. Stripped of them, naked, but beautiful and shimmering with oil, She entered Her sister's royal hall.

There sat Her sister, Erishkegal, Queen of Darkness, on her black throne. On either side stood Her advisers.

The beautiful, shining Queen of Heaven walked to the foot of the throne.

"What do You want here?" Erishkegal demanded.

Inanna looked up at Her Sister, and said, "Your throne, Sister.

Come down from there. Come down now."

"I rule here. The Dark Land was given to Me."

"I want it, and shall have it. I am Queen of Heaven. The Queen of Heaven should rule everywhere, don't you think? Come down from there now!"

Erishkegal rose, and descended the steps of Her throne. She stood with her counsellors and watched Inanna climb the steps and sit in the throne-chair.

Erishkegal turned to her seven counsellors, and said, "My Sister lives, but She has come into the Land of the Dead, against the laws. The throne of the Dead was given to Me, but She has taken it. What is your verdict on Her?"

The seven counsellors looked up at Inanna. One said, "We cannot speak to You except with the speech of Anger!"

Another said, "We must shout at You, with a shout of Guilt!"

Their leader said, "We can look at You only with the look of Death."

"Guilt and Death," said Erishkegal, Queen of Darkness. Holding Her own wand of polished black ebony, she walked up the steps, and struck Inanna. "Die."

Inanna did not flinch from the blow, but She had given up all Her Divine Powers. Without their protection, She fell dead.

Erishkegal, Queen of Darkness, took Her throne again. She had Her sister's body hung on hooks from the wall, and left it there.

In the bright world above, three days passed and Innanna did not return.

Ninshkurbur remembered her orders, and mourned for Inanna, rubbing dirt into her face and hair, and dressing in a single stained garment, like a poor woman. In ruined houses, she raised her voice in lament, and in the temple sanctuaries she beat a drum. She cut herself above the eyes, she cut her nose, she cut her ears, and let the blood run.

All alone she went to the God-House of Enlil. Before His altar she cried, "Oh Father Enlil, don't let Your Daughter be killed in the Underworld! Don't let Your precious metal be mixed with dirt there. Don't let Your lovely lapis-lazuli be split there along with mason's building stone. Don't let your scented box-wood be chopped up along with carpenter's wood. Don't let young Lady Inanna be killed in the Underworld."

How did Inanna's Father, the great God Enlil, answer? He said, "My Daughter had the Heavens, and she wanted the Great Below too. She knew that the Underworld is never left by those who enter it. She knew this, yet still She went there. She has Her wish— let Her be happy with it! I cannot help Her."

Ninshkurbur went to the temple of Nanna. There she made her plea before Nanna's altar: "Don't let young Lady Inanna be killed in the Underworld."

How did the Great God, Nanna, answer? He said, "Inanna had the Heavens, and She wanted the Underworld too. Now She has Her place there, and there She must stay. I cannot help Her."

Ninshkurbur went to the temple of Enki. Before His altar she made her plea: "Don't let young Lady Inanna be killed in the Underworld."

How did Enki the Wise answer? He said, "Oh, what has Inanna done now? She has Me worried. What has the Queen of Heaven done? Oh, that Girl worries Me. What is the Mistress of All Lands up to now? She worries Me, She does. I shall do all I can, all I can."

Enki gave much thought to the problem of saving Inanna. He scraped some dirt from beneath the nails on His left hand, and from the dirt He created a lovely creature, that was neither man nor woman, and He called it 'Gala-Tura'. He scraped dirt from beneath the nails of His right hand, and created another lovely creature, neither man nor woman, and He called it, 'Kur-Jara'.

To Kur-Jara, Enki gave the Life-Giving Flower. To Gala-Tura, he gave Life's Water.

"Listen to me," He said to them. "Go now to The Land of No Return. You must bring back the young Lady Inanna. Slip past the gates like little flies. Drift through the doors like ghosts. Find the Underworld's Queen, Erishkegal. She can never leave that dreary place, and is full of care and misery. Be kind to Her. When She says, 'Oh My head,' you must say, 'Oh Your head, poor Mistress.' When She says, 'Oh My heart,' you must say, 'Oh, Your poor heart, poor Mistress.' Do you understand?"

Gala-Tura and Kur-Jara nodded, wide-eyed.

"Good," said Enki. "Erishkegal will say, 'Who are you? You are so kind, I want to make you a gift.' Now, She may offer you many fine things, but whatever She offers you, refuse! You must say, 'We want nothing but that corpse hanging over there on the wall.' Do you understand?"

Again, they nodded.

"Excellent! Now, when you have the corpse you, Kur-Jara, must rub it with the juice of the Life-Giving Flower; and you, Gala-Tura, must sprinkle it with Life's Water. Then Inanna will arise."

So Gala-Tura, carrying a flask of the Life's Water, and Kur-Jara, carrying the Life Giving Flower, turned their steps towards the Land of No Return. Hand in hand, they walked down that steep path, into the dust and the dark.

When they reached the City of the Dead, they did as Enki had told them. They slipped past the gates like tiny flies. Through all the many doors of the Palace they passed like ghosts. They went into the royal hall, and found Erishkegal lying on a couch, sick and listless. It is a weary thing to be Queen of Darkness, never to leave the Underworld, and eating nothing but dry clay.

Gala-Tura and Kur-Jara sat by Her and smiled.

"Oh My head," She said. "It aches."

"Oh, poor Mistress," they said. "Oh, Your poor head!"

"But not as My heart aches," She said. "Oh, the ache I have there!"

"Oh, Your poor heart! Poor Mistress!"

"I am troubled," She said. "Sore troubled."

"Oh You are troubled! Poor Mistress!"

Erishkegal smiled. Not often did She hear such kind words. "And My back... And My sides..."

"Oh poor Mistress! Oh, Your poor back! Oh, Your poor sides!"

"Sweet creatures!" She said. "What can I give you to make you happy? What would you like? I see you carry water— would you like a whole river?"

"No Mistress."

"A lake? A sea?"

"Oh, no Mistress."

"Your friend, then? You carry a flower, dear creature. Would you like a whole field of flowers?"

"Oh no Mistress!"

"Then what would you like? Tell me."

Both of them pointed to the corpse that hung on the wall behind the couch.

"Oh, no," said Erishkegal. "You don't want that thing! Let Me give you a country or two!"

They shook their heads.

"What then? What would you like?"

They pointed to the corpse.

Erishkegal was bored. "Oh, take it then," She said, and went away.

Gala-Tura and Kur-Jara knelt by the body. They rubbed it with the juice of the Life Giving Flower, and they sprinkled it with Life's Water. The corpse stirred, it drew breath, and Inanna climbed down from the hooks where she hung on the wall. More juice and more water healed the wounds made by the hooks. Inanna stood, naked, fresh and beautiful as ever.

Inanna took the hand of Gala-Tura, She took the hand of Kur-Jara, and with them She walked from the palace. She set Her mind on the World Above, and turned Her steps towards it.

Then, clattering from all sides, came Demons, the guardians of Erishkegal's palace and the Land of Darkness. They said, "You may not, You cannot, leave. None has ever come into this Land of Darkness, and left."

Inanna said, "I am the Queen of Heaven, and I come and go as I please. I come into the Underworld, and I leave it again."

"You may not," said the demons. "Those who enter our world can never leave. We cannot say to our Queen, 'We had so many, and now we have one less.'"

"If You go from here," said the demons, "You must send another in Your place. We must keep count."

"Who will take Your place?" asked the demons. "Who in the world above will leave the sunlight, come down into cold and darkness and take Your place?"

Inanna left the Underworld and walked up into the sunlight again, but a great Demon trod before Her, carrying a sceptre; and a great Demon trod behind Her, carrying a mace; and all around Her, and behind Her, and on each side of Her, walked small demons, like a fence. She could not escape.

These demons of the Underworld, they never eat, they never drink. They never accept gifts. They never know a warm hug, or a sweet kiss. But to fill their dark land, they will snatch a little son from his father's knee, they will snatch a bride from her wedding-feast, a man from his wife's embrace, they will take a baby from its mother.

As they left the Underworld, as they came into the sun, Ninshkurbur was waiting, on her knees, dressed in one filthy garment, her face cut and bleeding.

"Here is one," said the demons to Inanna. "We'll take her in Your place."

"By no means!" said Inanna. "This is my faithful minister. She did not forget Me. She lamented for Me, she went from God's house to God's house for Me. Because of her, I am returned to the Sun. Never shall I give her to you." Lifting Ninshkurbur to her feet, She hugged her. "We shall go on!"

They walked on, surrounded by demons, and entered a city. At the gate, Cara knelt, waiting, dressed in dirty clothes, with dirt in his hair and on his face.

"Here is one," said the demons. "Go on Your way, Inanna. We

will take him."

"You shall not!" cried Inanna. "Cara has mourned for Me, and is waiting for Me. You shall not have him!" She lifted Cara up and hugged him, and went on with him and Ninshkurbur, with demons all around them.

They went on, and met with Lulal, dressed in dirty clothes and lamenting Inanna's death.

"Here is one!" said the demons. "We will take this one."

"Lulal, My youngest son?"Inanna said. "Never! He has mourned for Me, and you shall not have him."

"We go on," said the demons; and on they all went.

They entered Inanna's palace and walked through it to the pleasant gardens. There, sheltering from the heat under a cool, scented apple tree, was Dumuzi, Inanna's husband and lord.

Had he dressed himself in dirty clothes to mourn for his Wife? No. He was dressed in magnificent clothes of fine linen decorated with beads, and gold fringes.

Was he sitting in the dust, had he rubbed dirt into his hair and face to mourn Her? No. He was seated in a throne, eating figs and drinking milk mixed with honey.

Was he lamenting for Her loss? No. He was playing on the flute to amuse himself.

Inanna cried out to him, "How can you sit in the shade, eating and drinking and enjoying yourself, when I have been hung on hooks, hung on a wall, a corpse?" It was the shout of Anger.

Inanna snatched the flute from him, She upset the milk and honey, scattered the figs. "How can you be happy when I have been in the Land of Darkness?" It was the shout of Guilt.

She stood back and looked at Dumuzi, Her husband. It was the look of Death. She said to the demons, "Take him in My place."

The demons seized Dumuzi, and was carried him away into the Land of Darkness, to the City of the Dead.

Inanna was glad. She gloried in the sunlight and warmth, in the taste of milk, honey and figs.

But when night came, She missed Dumuzi. She wept and tore at Her hair, crying, "Where is My man? What have I done?" For though Dumuzi had angered Her, he was beautiful, and She loved him.

And because Inanna wept and lay sleepless at night, and grieved all day, the corn withered, and the leaves fell from the trees. The air was chilled, and life in the World Above was harsh.

Dumuzi's sister, Geshtinanna, came to the palace, crying, "Why are you so cruel, Lady? Why have you sent my brother into the Dead Land? It breaks my heart into pieces to know that I shall never see him again. I wish the Earth might be barren and fruitless forever, since my brother is dead."

Inanna embraced Geshtinanna, and sat with her by a brazier of coals. "He made Me angry, but now I am sorry. I cry all day because he is not here, and all night too. I am love-sick and weary— but there is no help for it. No one can leave the Land of Darkness unless another is ready to take their place."

Geshtinanna said, "I will take his place."

"What are you saying?" said Inanna. "Will you go into that land of Darkness, where there is no warmth, and all is dry dust; where nothing is eaten but clay and nothing is drunk; where there are no embraces and no kisses— you would go there for your brother's sake?"

"I will share his unhappiness. I will take his place in the City of the Dead for half the year, so that he can live a little while under the Sun... I will do this if he will return to the Underworld and take my place there for the year's other half. For his sake, for him only, I will give up half my life, so that he can live it."

Inanna embraced her and wept. "You are good, you are brave, and I love you."

When half the year had passed, in cold barrenness, Inanna and Geshtinanna walked hand in hand to the gates of the Underworld, and knocked. Inanna said to the gatekeeper, "Here is Dumuzi's sister, who is willing to take his place. Let him come out to us. And in six months time, let the demons come and demand his presence in the

Underworld, and release Geshtinanna."

So it was done. Geshtinanna, that brave and loving girl, entered the Underworld, and Dumuzi left behind the Land of Darkness, and walked hand in hand with Inanna back into the sun. And as they walked together, the air and land warmed, the leaves sprang green on the trees, and the shoots sprang green in the fields. Inanna was glad again, because Dumuzi was returned to Her, and Her joy warmed the whole Earth.

Six months passed, the corn grew, the trees fruited, and the harvest was gathered. Then the demons came from the Underworld. "Now," they said, "Dumuzi must return."

Inanna held tight to him, She cried, She begged, but there was no help for it. Dumuzi was led back to the Underworld by the demons. As he entered its gate, His sister, Geshtinanna, left it, and returned to the world above.

Inanna welcomed Geshtinanna, but could not hide Her grief. Six months, a long half-year, without Dumuzi stretched before Her, and Her grief was fiercer than before. The air chilled. Leaves fell, grass died. Water froze.

Every year, since that time, when the demons call Dumuzi to the Underworld, the women of the world join Inanna in Her grieving. They cut their hair, rub dust and ashes in it, and dress themselves in dirty clothes. They scratch and cut their faces, and wail and scream their grief in the streets. And Winter comes.

Every year, when the gates of the Underworld open, and Dumuzi is released, then the women of the world join Inanna in rejoicing. They paint their eyes, redden their lips and cheeks. They dress themselves in their finest clothes and jewels, and scatter flowers in the streets, while singing and dancing. And Summer comes.

## AUTHOR'S NOTE.ON 'THE QUEEN OF HEAVEN VISITS THE QUEEN OF DARKNESS.'

I didn't know this story before I was asked, by a children's publisher, to make it one of the stories in a collection of myths of the underworld. I duly researched it, and was delighted with the humour and sensuality of this ancient tale— it's Sumerian, one of the oldest civilisations on earth.

I particularly liked Enki's worried fretting— "Oh that girl, what has she done?"— which isn't my invention. It's in the original myth, as is the sweet-talking of Erishkegal— "Oh poor you, oh your poor head."

When I submitted the story, the publisher— who evidently hadn't read the myth before either— found it too sexual and too violent for children. I took out all reference to Inanna's being naked after she passes through the seven gates. Readers, I said, could imagine her naked or, if they pleased, dress her in undercrackers of their choice, whether Janet Reger or voluminous bloomers and vest. The text no longer gave them any direction. I also changed the body being hung on a hook— as it is in the myth— to being 'thrown into a corner'.

No good. The story was turned down, and remained unpublished. Which is why it appears here.

# MISSING THE BUS

A night of city lights leaned on the windows: a siren doplared. Far off and close by, telephones rang.

"Hello, Bus-Aid!" Almost yawning, heaving up brightness from the weariness. "How can I help you?"

"Is that the busht, buzz— ah— bus place?" Dim telephonic laughter behind the voice, coughing, glass chimes.

"This is Bus-Aid, yes. How can I help you?"

"Gotta get my, my kid— get my kid to school."

"It's ten-forty, madam. At night."

"Gotta go to shchool." A murmur, off. "Tomorrow, yeah. Tomorrow morning. School."

"Where do you want to catch the bus from from, and where are you going to?"

"What?" Intense puzzlement.

"Where do you want to catch the bus and where are you going?"

"Smy kid, not me. My kid cashing."

"Yes, madam, but where do you want them to catch the bus, and where are they going?"

Silence. In the ear, a muffled, distant scream of laughter, a crisp packet rustle.

Before the eyes, the computer keyboard, the computer screen. Colleagues at other desks, pale in the office lights, faces flickering with computer reflections. City lights and rain on the dark windows.

"Madam? Are you there?"

A grunt, and a male voice. "Sorry mate. Her's well pissed, this one. Trying to find out a bus for her kid tomorrow morning."

"Yes, but where does the kid want to catch the bus, do you know? Can you ask her?"

"It'll be Shire Oak, mate. Her lives near there."

"And where's the school?"

"Oh, I dunno. Where's the school? Mags! Where's the school? Her's gone! Anybody know where her kid goes to school? Don't know, mate."

"I'm sorry, I can't help unless I know— " A burr, the call ended.

Immediately, another ring. "Bus-Aid! How can I help— ?"

"I'm outside Green Dragon. When's the bus to the Coach?"

"The Green Dragon public house in Hoffman Street?"

"Dunno mate— oh! Ar! There's a sign over there. Hoffman Street. Never saw that before."

"And you want to go to the Coach? Is that its full name?"

"Its full name?"

"Is it called 'The Coach,' or is 'The Coach and Horses,' or 'The Stage Coach,' or— "

"The Coach and Horses, mate. Wakeman Street."

"There's the 81 in— "

"It used to be my local, y'know."

"Yeah? In about ten minutes, the— "

"It's a bloody jungle outpost now. No English she spokee here. Even the bloody barman's foreign."

"The 81— "

"Hitler had the right idea, dinny? You reckon?"

"Sir— "

"My daughter might get a council house if Hitler was in charge. That's right, innit?"

90

"Sir, do you— ?"

"Oh, it's coming. The bus. It's here. Tara!"

Call ended.

"Bus-Aid! Stuck here all night, crying out to the wilderness."

"Eh?"

"How can I help you?"

"You can tell me where the fucking 72 is and don't be smart."

"Where are you calling from, sir?"

"From the fucking 72 stop, where'd you think? Only there's no 72. Been stood here half a fucking hour and no fucking bus and I'm freezing me fucking balls off so don't give me no lip."

"Which, of all the many 72 stops, are you at, sir?"

"Are you going to tell me where it is or not?"

"Are you going to tell me which 72 stop you're at?"

"I said don't be smart."

"Sir, you're being very abusive— "

"And you're being a dick-head."

"Our company policy is— "

"Oh, go on, I ask for a bus and you give me some fucking guff—

"

" —that if you continue being abusive— "

"You'll what? What you going to do?"

"Cut you off."

"You fucking— " Call ended.

Calls rose up through the darkness to the illuminated tower.

"What's happened to the one-five-four to Galton Green? I'm at Galton Bridge."

"Should be with you in a moment, Madam. There's a bus out of service on that route, and they are running a little late."

"Oh, okay— g'night!"

"Good night, Madam.— Bus-Aid! How may I help you?"

"Please, I want to know a bus."

"Certainly. Can we start with where you're calling from?"

"Where? You?"

"Where are you calling from, please, sir?"

"Calling from? Please?"

"Where are you calling from? Can you tell me? Where are you? Where are you now?"

"Er... I am... Norra— Norrafarluck."

"*Where?*"

"Narrafalluk."

"I'm not familiar... Can you spell it?"

"Spelleet?"

"Never mind. Do you know the post-code?"

"Post-cod?"

"Oh, for— I don't have anything on the computer that looks like that, sir. You say you're in Narrafalluk? Is that a street name? A town name? A district name?"

"Nor-witch!"

"Sorry?"

"Nor-witch in Narrafalluk!"

"Norwich? Is that Norwich? You're in Norwich in Norfolk?"

"Yes! I want to know a bus!"

"Sir... I'm in Birmingham."

"Hello— good evening."

"No, sir— you're two hundred miles away. We don't cover Norfolk. But hang on, I'll see if I can— "

"You tell me bus?"

"I'm sorry, sir, no, but— if I can find the number of the Norfolk— "

"No bus?"

"If I can find the number of the Norfolk— "

"Okay. Is fine. No bus."

Call ended.

"I could have put you through! I was trying to put you through! Now you're standing there in some dark sheep-shagging lane in deepest Norfolk— Oh, give me strength!" Phone rings. "Bus-Aid! How may I help you?— Yes, madam, if you walk down to the Hayley

Road, you'll have a choice of two buses within the next twenty minutes, the nine-eleven, and the two-thirteen."

"Thanks, lad, you're a star. On lates tonight, then?"

"I work nights, madam."

"What, every night? Not much of a life is it, that?"

"It's okay. Can I help you with anything else, madam?"

"Oh, you're ever so polite. I'm thinking of getting a take-away. There's a few along here, d'you know 'em? There's burgers, and chicken and Indian— what would you have?"

"I don't know, madam. Is that all you want to know? About the buses?"

"My son'd have a burger, every time. He loved a burger. He lives down on the South Coast now. Married one of them Peculiar People— you know them? Don't suppose he sees many burgers now, not with her."

"Madam— "

"Very religious. Won't let him have anything to do with me, cos I aint one of 'em. They got two sons— my grandsons. I never see 'em. Do you think that's right?"

"I can't say, madam. I can only tell you the bus time-table."

"But can that be right? Religious people— well, they say they're religious— splitting up families? I never see me grandsons, me husband's dead. Can that be right?"

"I can only help you with the bus and train timetables, madam."

"You're a good lad."

"Thank you, madam."

"Good night then."

"Good night.— Bus— "

"Iss zat bus plaishe?"

"Yes, Madam, it's Bus-Aid. How can I help?"

"Bus f'ma kid."

"Excuse me?"

"Want a bus for me kid!"

"Where is your kid travelling from, madam?"

"Where's he— ? He's going to school!"

"Yes, madam, but he'll be travelling from home? Where do you live? Where will your son be travelling from?"

"Douglas Road."

"Hanley?"

"Eh?"

"Is that Douglas Road, Hanley?"

"I told you, didn't I? He's got to get shchool. They'll be after me 'gain, he don't get school."

"And where is his school? Where is his school, madam? That he'll be travelling to? Madam? Madam!"

"Uh! What?"

"Please try to stay awake, madam, and we'll get this sorted. Where is the school he'll be travelling to?"

"What school?"

"The school your son goes to, madam?— This is Bus-Aid, madam. We were trying to find a bus for your son to travel to school by tomorrow."

A sigh, and a snore.

"Madam! We will be closing soon. If you want to settle this... Can you tell me the name of your son's school?"

"I dunno what— Itsh by— woss it called. Call it 'Parrot'. 'Saa pub."

"The Perrot Arms, madam?"

"Thassit."

"That's Perrot Road, madam. Would your son's school be the Perrot Road School? Does that ring a bell?"

"Perra. Row. Shchoo."

"Is that where your son goes?"

"Oh. Yeah. If you say so."

"If— Madam, where are you now?"

"What?"

"Where are you? Where are you speaking from?"

"Outside pub. In a car outside pub."

"You're not driving, are you?"

"Nah. Can't drive."

"And where's your son?"

"He's got to getta school."

"The 801 from Hanley Road at eight-twenty will get him to Perrot Road by eight-fifty."

"Right."

"The 801, Madam, got that? Eight-twenty. Madam?— Madam?"

Indistinct noises: scratchings, shufflings, sighs. End call.

The voices rise up to the lights of the tower.

"Where's the bus? Have I missed it?"

"Is there a bus at— "

"Are the buses running tonight?"

"Will the bus be here soon?"

"Have I missed the bus?"

Even when the lights are turned out, and the tower is dark, the calls beat against its brick and glass. Echoing in the empty office, the phones ring.

"When's the last bus?"

"The bus should be here."

"Have I missed the bus?"

*Author's Note on 'Missing The Bus.'*

This isn't a ghost story, or supernatural in any way, but I find the image of a half-lit tower rising up from the darkness of a big city, clamourous with disembodied voices begging for direction, quite haunting in its way.

A friend once did the work described here— answering phone-calls about bus and train timetables. The conversations in the story are all based on conversations my friend had— though condensed into a short read rather than spread out over several months.

# OVERHEARD IN A MUSEUM

When the doors of the hall open, I smell the sea. I hear its roar. The pulse of the long-felled oak runs through me, and I feel the sea rush past and under me. I surge forward to climb the wave. But I never move. I shall never more move.

The people pass either side of me, staring. They touch me, though the guards forbid it.

Quite still, I rest in my cradle. But every part of me— my ribs, my spine, my breast-bone— strains after the sea and the whale's path, the gull's track, that I once rode.

A thousand years ago, before I ever was, I was in dreams. People saw me in their minds and wanted me.

My master dreamed of me so long, and longed for me so sharply, that he laid by timber in open sheds, to weather. He laid by gold and silver, to pay for my building. He bought iron, in blocks and rods, for the making of my nails and rivets.

He knew I would be costly. He knew he would need to call together shipwrights and carpenters, blacksmiths and rope-makers. Skilful men like that do not work for nothing, and they must be fed and housed while they work.

But my master had land, and slaves and full barns. He had his gold, silver and iron. I was a rich man's dream. In his mind, always, he saw me. He sent out a call for his ship-wrights and blacksmiths. He set men searching the forests for an oak tall enough and thick enough to be my spine.

What was his name? I shall not say. He was a tall man, taller than many others, wealthy, and respected. Now he is bones.

I remain.

The men took my master to the tree they'd found. A great forest oak, four times as high as a house. An old, old tree, full of life and strength. My master ordered it felled. The hard sound of the axes hacking at the trunk flew from the mountainside and over the fjord far below. The crash of the falling tree was louder.

The oak was dragged, by horses and men, to the shore, where they set it up on stocks to be my heart, my backbone, my keel. All the oak's strength and life became mine.

The shipwrights and the blacksmiths set to work. The blacksmiths sweated and hammered in hot forges, to turn the iron rods into nails and rivets. The shipwrights shaped blocks of wood into my stern-post and bow-post. They fastened them to either end of my keel, with wooden pegs, and with long iron nails. I smelled, then, of fresh cut wood, and fire and hot iron— and of the nearby sea. My making was mirrored in the water of the fjord, and above the hammering of the black-smiths and the shipwrights, the gulls screamed.

More trees were felled. Men split them lengthways, with wedges and axes, into planks. My master came to watch when the first planks were fastened to my keel with more long iron nails. The first row of planking along my keel, that was the first strake. The second strake was laid to overlap the first, and between the two rows of planks was pressed thick cord soaked in tar, to make all water-tight. Then the overlapping planks were riveted tight together with iron rivets.

Oh, said the people, who passed by— so much iron going into that ship! So much iron that could be used to make ploughs, or axes, or a thousand more useful things. So much work, so much cost. It's not made of wood, that ship, they said. It's made of gold, silver and sweat.

I am a rich man's dream.

Nine strakes they fastened along my keel. The sea-waves come to shore in nine waves, so I heard men say. Eight waves, and then the ninth is bigger. Eight waves more, and then the ninth. Nine— a magical number.

To make me, skilled men burned stone and turned it to metal. To make me, trees gave up their lives. I was magical.

Nine strakes they laid, and they knew that would be my water-line. So there they fixed in my ribs, where I needed to be strong against the sea. Nineteen ribs of oak I had, and they were all one metre apart. My crew would sit between my ribs to row, and a rowing man needs a metre of space.

They were not fastened to my keel, these ribs, but only to the planking. I am not a man, to have my ribs fastened to my spine! I outlived the man who dreamed me, and all the men who made me.

More strakes were added now, to cover my ribs, but these planks were thicker, for against them the sea would strike and they must be strong. And here I'll tell you of the cleverness of these men who made me. They drilled holes through my ribs, and through the strakes, and they passed lashings through the holes and so lashed my ribs to my skin of planking. They used no iron in nails or rivets here, but the tough, springy roots of spruce trees, and the thin, twistable whale-bone from the mouths of whales. So my sides were not fixed and rigid, but as flexible and sinuous as a snake.

At the ninth strake my cross-beams were fitted too, from rib to rib, right across my width, increasing my strength.

And then, strake on strake, all caulked with twine dipped in tar, and riveted to each other, and lashed to my ribs, until there were sixteen strakes. In the topmost strake the carpenters fashioned round holes through which my oars would be pushed, when they were needed, or drawn back in when I moved before the wind. Each hole had a small shutter, so it could be closed against the sea. All measured and cut, just so, with the greatest of skill.

But my mast, my mast. At my very centre, resting on my keel, was a great block of oak. A deep socket was hollowed in it, and that socket held the foot of my tall mast.

Above this, they placed another oaken block, with a slot cut into it, from the side to the middle. Many men heaved on ropes twisted from strips of walrus hide, and heaved up my mast, until its foot slipped into the socket in the bottom-most block. Up, up came the mast, and was tugged into the slot in the uppermost block. And, when it was upright, they hammered a plug of oak into the slot— sweated and hammered— until the mast was tightly wedged. They braced the mast with more ropes made of arctic walrus hide.

Now my master came every day, and walked about me and looked at me with pride, for I was beautiful, and almost finished.

"What shall I call her?" my master asked, and the men who worked about me called out.

"Wind-Raven! She'll fly before the wind like a bird— she should be named for Odin's bird."

"No— Sea-Stag. Or Sea-Deer. She'll be fast as a deer."

"Sea-Snake. She should be Sea-Snake, because she'll glide through the water like a snake."

"Dark Stallion," said another.

"Horse of the Ice-Home."

They brought my steer-board and fitted it to my side, and so harnessed and reined me, like any horse.

They put in my decking planks, and fitted the rack to my gunwales, where my men would hang their shields. They painted me, in stripes of red and white, and they gilded the animal's head carved on my tiller. My sail was fetched, from the hall where the women had been weaving and sewing it— so much work went into my making! The sail was square and, like my hull, was striped red and white.

Then the carved head for my prow was carried down from the house of the master woodcarver, and fixed at my prow. It was the snarling head of an animal with an arched neck that might have been a dragon, or might have been a horse, and it was brightly painted, and gilded.

All the people who had worked on me gathered to see me finished: all the carpenters, and rope-makers, all the women who had woven the sail, all the painters, and they all cheered to see me completed at last, and so beautiful.

"What is she to be called?" they asked my master.

My master carried a lamb under his arm, and he came to stand close beside me, at my prow. He cut the lamb's throat, spraying blood on my breast and keel, and he shouted aloud to everyone the name he had chosen for me.

The warm blood splashed on my strakes, my name was spoken, and I shuddered on my cradle and groaned as my spirit woke in me, in every part, from the oaken strength of my keel to the tree-height of my mast. But I shall not tell the name my master chose. They are all gone, those who knew my name, and now I am called by another, which was never mine. My true name, with its luck and power, shall stay my secret.

I slid from my cradle, slid down the strand, and into the water. There I floated, a great, fierce bird, bright of colouring, glittering. My master came on board, with his men, and they took their places on the benches and put out their oars. I took the water and the water took me. Out I moved, into the deep water, under the steep mountains. The oars struck the water, and the men roared together. Around me the water spangled, sparkled, glittered, brighter than gold or gems. I sang, for the first time, as the wind hummed in my ropes, as my sides flexed and my mast groaned, as the oars pivoted in their holes, as my master shifted the steer-board.

"She is a beauty!" my master called out, and the men cheered. That was a great day, but better still was the day I first left the shelter of the mountains and entered the open sea. How the waves dashed against my sides— and how I leaped to meet them! How the sea opened, an endless stretch of bright water and far sky. My prow, my golden dragon's head, strained for the horizon.

That was the first day my sail was raised, and the oars drawn in. I dashed against the waves, climbed them, dived them. They smashed against me with great blows— spray flew. Along my length my sides gave to them and sprang back. My prow twisted, to the right, to the left as I followed my scent, and my long length writhed through the water like a snake. My sail, spread like a wing, took the wind and thrust me on. Like a valkyrie I shrieked, as the wind thrummed my ropes; and all my timbers groaned.

My master leaned over my side, slapping my bulwarks. "She is fast— fast!" Truly, I earned the name he gave me, a thousand years ago.

The Spring Viking!— when the fields have been ploughed and the seed planted. Then my master left his lands in the care of old men, and he and his crew pushed me to the water and sailed to fight for kings and earn gold. I brought them back when the seed had grown into tall barley, ready for harvesting— but when it was cut, and safe in the barn, then was the time for the Fall Viking, before the winter storms.

I carried my master over the Gull's Tracks, to the Hilt-Islands, to the Whale-Islands, to the Southern Islands, and to the land of the Angles. I learned to know the great swells of the North Sea, and the wilder Atlantic waters, as I breasted the big waves, and climbed and rode them, and dived into their hollows. I ran my keel up many beaches, the shingle screeching beneath me, and my men splashed down into the water and to wade ashore. Sometimes they lit a fire to warm themselves and cook. Often enough they lit a fire to warm others, for the last time. I was no fat-bellied trading ship. Look at me. I am built like a sword.

I was in battles fought in narrow inlets, and my sides are scarred by the iron grapples thrown from other ships, to hold my hull tight against theirs, while the arrows flew like angry, stinging bees, and axes hacked and spears jabbed. Blood stained my decks, but I don't bleed.

Still, ships grow old and wear out, as men do. My master and I grew old together, and when my master died, I was an old ship. My master had a long journey, to the land of the dead. How else should he go but in the ship he loved?

I was dragged, by men and horses, from the shore to a hill with a view to the fjord. There a grave had been dug, down through the earth and into the clay, and into the clay I was dragged.

There I settled, far from the sea.

A bed was set up, at my stern; and my master's body was laid on the bed, close to my steer-board. So often had he taken my tiller and held my steer-board against the weight of the sea, guiding me as a rider guides a horse.

His people boarded me, bringing his weapons: his shield, his spear, his sword, laying them by him on the bed. They brought him food, and jars of ale and wine, placing them near him.

They brought on board everything he would need when he had sailed far from them. A sled, for travelling in winter; and harness for horses. Cauldrons and pots for cooking, chests for storage. Blankets and cloaks. Benches and wall-hangings, a chessboard and chessmen, for the hall he would find at his journey's end.

They brought his six dogs on board, killed them, and laid them near him. The dogs struggled and howled when they smelt the blood of their fellows, but they were all killed.

Twelve horses they led into the grave, and though the horses were nervous and fought and kicked, they killed them all and laid them around my hull.

Then the men filled in the grave. They threw earth and sand and clay, piling it up about my hull, and throwing it inside me. I was filled. My prow, my stern-post sank in earth, and earth closed over me, as the sea had never done. I was sealed into darkness.

A thousand years' sleep.

I dreamed a long sailing, through green waters, into light, and another shore that waited there...

My sides were never broken by the sea, but they bent, cracked and splintered beneath the weight of earth and stones.

The dream broke, light returned. The grave opened.

Men working with wheelbarrows and with shovels carried the earth away from me. My hiding place was opened to the sky.

I was wreckage, crushed, all my beauty and strength gone. My master's bones lay among my broken ribs.

But still men dreamed of me. They lifted up my ribs, they gathered my splinters, my broken strakes, my corroded, rusted nails. Not a piece of me was left in the grave.

Again, the men of craft gathered, and worked on me with all their skill. Again my keel was laid, and my strakes fixed. Again I was built, with as much love and hope as before.

And I was set here, in this long white hall. My mast is gone, and so are my bright colours. The gilded head from my prow rotted in the grave. My unknown name will never be spoken again. My master, too, is gone from me. I am empty.

But still I am beautiful, the long sweep and lines of me.

When the doors of the hall open, I smell the sea. I hear it. The pulse of the long-felled oak runs through me, and I feel the sea rush past and under me, and I surge forward to climb the wave. But I never move. I shall never more move.

Until this white hall falls, here I shall stay. I have outlived the men who made me. I have outlived the men who dug me from the grave.

I shall outlive you, who overhear me. I shall outlive many, many more; and I shall race my keel through the dreams of many.

But never again will the sea be under me. Never again the Gull's Track.

# AUTHOR'S NOTE ON 'OVERHEARD IN A MUSEUM.'

The overheard ship is the Gokstad, which can be seen in the Viking Ship Museum in Oslo, Norway. It is called 'the Gokstad' after the place where it was found buried, in 1880, but that was not its name.

The ship was built in around 900 AD. In length it was seventy-six and a half feet (23.24 metres), and its width was seventeen and a half feet (5.20 metres).

The depth, from its gunwale to the bottom of its keel was less than six and a half feet (2 metres).

Its keel was fifty-eight feet (17.50 metres) long and was made of a single oak-tree.

The Gokstad was a war-ship, and probably carried a crew of somewhere between thirty-two and sixty-four men, as thirty-two shields, painted yellow and black, were found along each side.

The man buried in the 'Gokstad' was aged between fifty and sixty, and, when alive, had been over six feet tall (over 1 metre 80). His identity can never be known for certain, but it has been suggested that he was King Olaf Gudroddsson, of Vestfold and Geirstad, who died at roughly the right time and place to be the man buried in the ship.

Grave goods were buried with him, for his voyage to the other world, including the dogs and horses mentioned in the story— and a peacock!

After his death King Olaf was worshipped as an elf, and became known as 'Olaf Geirstad-Alf'— the elf of Geirstad.

I have always been fascinated by the Norse Myths and the Viking Age. From my teens, I had an ambition to visit Oslo's Viking Ship Museum, and see the Gokstad and the other magnificent ship housed there, the Oseberg.

When I did make the trip, I spent four hours in the museum, while other tourists whipped round in ten minutes. I was there so long, I attracted the suspicion of a guard, who hovered near me, afraid, I think, that I was suddenly going to take a hammer to the ships.

I reassured him, and he then gave me something of a tour, pointing out small details.

The idea for this story came after I'd written the story that opens this collection, 'Overheard In A Graveyard.' In that story I'd honed the tale down to a dialogue. Why not give the Gokstad a voice, to tell its own story?

The 'Article' section on my website gives a link to a piece I wrote about the Oseberg ship — a ship just as beautiful as the Gokstad and in many ways even more mysterious.

# ABOUT THE AUTHOR

Susan Price's is a British author who gained her first publishing contract, with Faber and Faber, at the age of sixteen.

Since then, she has won the Carnegie Medal for the 'modern classic' The Ghost Drum, and the Guardian Prize for The Sterkarm Handshake.
Both have attracted the attention of film companies.

In 2011, she was one of the first British authors to begin self-publishing e-books and, now, paperbacks.
She is a founder, together with her friend and fellow writer, Katherine Roberts, of the multi-blog Authors Electric.

Find it at: http://authorselectric.blogspot.com

Susan Price's own website can be found at:

**www.susanpriceauthor.com**

She blogs at Susan Price's Nennius Blog:

**http://susanpricesblog.blogspot.co.uk/**

www.ingramcontent.com/pod-product-compliance
Lightning Source LLC
Chambersburg PA
CBHW072010170626
46813CB00005B/2098